Rand's blue ... **proposing to me?**

"I know that's typically a man's domain," Ginger replied.

He smiled. "You think I'd take my sweet time about it, is that it?"

He certainly took his sweet time about a lot of things. In bed, anyway. Ginger flushed, disturbed that the only way they knew each other all that well was sensually.

She waved off his assertion. "Don't know. Don't care." She stuck her hat back on her head. "I just want a ring on my finger before any more time elapses. So that by the time I'm showing and we have to start telling people I'm pregnant, we'll already be married, and it won't be such a big deal."

His eyes never left hers as he stood there in that very still way that he had. "Oh, it's a big deal, all right," he said in a low, soft voice that sent ribbons of sensation coasting down her spine.

Dear Reader,

Life would be pretty boring if nothing *ever* changed. On the other hand, unexpected change often causes havoc in our personal and professional lives.

Such is the case for environmental engineer Rand McCabe and wildcatter Ginger Rollins. Neither plan to marry anytime soon. Never mind live in a honeymoon cottage with each other for the rest of the year! Yet unexpected circumstances quickly force them to do both.

And there the fun begins. Ginger vows sharing quarters with the sexy McCabe heartthrob will not alter her feelings or feisty, independent outlook in the slightest. For her, it's business first, last and always. The family-oriented Rand wants their relationship to grow into something much more satisfying, but only if the maddeningly elusive Ginger will let down her guard, and open up her heart.

Neither Ginger nor Rand understand that when life changes, they must change, too.

For more information on this and other books, please visit me at www.cathygillenthacker.com, and on Facebook and Twitter.

Best wishes, and happy reading!

Cathy Gillen Thacker

THE TEXAS WILDCATTER'S BABY

Cathy Gillen Thacker

HARLEQUIN® AMERICAN ROMANCE®

Recycling programs
for this product may
not exist in your area.

ISBN-13: 978-0-373-75510-3

THE TEXAS WILDCATTER'S BABY

Copyright © 2014 by Cathy Gillen Thacker

Printed in U.S.A.

ABOUT THE AUTHOR

Cathy Gillen Thacker is married and a mother of three. She and her husband spent eighteen years in Texas and now reside in North Carolina. Her mysteries, romantic comedies and heartwarming family stories have made numerous appearances on bestseller lists, but her best reward, she says, is knowing one of her books made someone's day a little brighter. A popular Harlequin author for many years, she loves telling passionate stories with happy endings, and thinks nothing beats a good romance and a hot cup of tea! You can visit Cathy's website, at www.cathygillenthacker.com, for more information on her upcoming and previously published books, recipes and a list of her favorite things.

Books by Cathy Gillen Thacker

HARLEQUIN AMERICAN ROMANCE

Chapter One

Whoever would have thought, Ginger Rollins wondered, that a tiny plus sign would have the power to forever change her life? But there it was. Bold as ever in the window of the testing device.

She sighed and stood, her knees wobbling as she paced the length of the nondescript hotel room she currently called home. Barely able to wrap her mind around the stunning news—she thought back to the rowdy town hall meeting in Summit, Texas, just six weeks ago. Where she'd locked eyes—and disputed ideas—with one tall, sexy, indomitable Texan.

If only her passionate arguing with Rand McCabe had ended there.

But no, as per usual whenever they met up, the two of them hadn't been able to call it quits when the meeting ended, and instead had taken their verbal clashing down the street to the establishment that stayed open the latest in that small mountain town. Equal parts pub, dance hall and pool parlor, the cavernous tavern was packed to the rafters with a singles-only event meant to take away the annual sting of Valentine's Day for the romantically unattached.

The band was loud, the company lively, the margaritas so strong you had to surrender your car keys and sign a pledge promising not to drink and drive to even get one.

If only, Ginger thought, she had stopped there, said a cool but firm good-night to Rand, and stuck to her usual ginger ale. Instead she had risen to the challenge of the ruggedly handsome environmentalist, and taken a seat beside him at the bar, where their disagreement had turned to laughter, their animosity to shameless flirting. Along with a host of others, they had closed the place down and taken the party bus back to her room at the Summit Inn.

The next thing Ginger knew sunlight had been streaming through the blinds. Her body still humming with the bone-deep satisfaction that was every bit as familiar to her as he was, she'd opened her eyes and groaned, aware it had happened. Again.

Only this time she had a scarlet heart with a broken arrow tattooed just below her shoulder. Rand had an exploding heart inked on *his* upper arm. And both of them were as naked as the day they were born. Ginger had moaned in dismay, because once again she'd felt way too exposed and vulnerable. "I don't believe this," she'd whispered to herself. *When would she ever learn?*

"Can't say I mind," a low masculine voice had drawled back.

Ginger winced. "Of course you don't mind," she'd muttered. He'd had a great time.

They both had.

"In fact, I don't think I've ever had a better Valentine's Day," he'd added.

As confident—and determined—as ever, Rand had turned his ruggedly handsome face and warm, strong body to hers. The stubble of morning beard, a shade darker than his rumpled mahogany hair, had lined his jaw. A sexy smile turned up the corners of his lips. But it was the compelling masculine intensity of his midnight-blue eyes when he'd admired her tousled hair and kiss-swollen lips that had really left her enthralled.

Damn him for reminding her just how right they were together. In bed anyway....

Ginger knew she should have said no when Rand's grin broadened and he'd reached for her again. Instead she'd given in to overwhelming desire and said yes to making love one last time.

To her relief, their coordinating tattoos hadn't been real. But apparently the consequences of their actions *had been*. And now, Ginger thought, on a fresh wave of emotion, she had to decide what to do before any more precious time elapsed.

RAND McCABE HAD collected eleven of the twelve soil samples he needed from in and around the Summit Creek bed when the pickup stopped just south of him. The door opened and an achingly familiar woman, with a mane of long copper-colored hair, stepped out into the warm spring sunshine.

A real looker, Ginger Rollins was dressed much like the last time he had seen her, in formfitting jeans, white T-shirt and button-up Western vest. Her leather boots were thick and sturdy, meant for traversing hard-scrabble ground. Her stone suede hat had a rolled brim that spoke volumes about her sassy attitude.

And while Rand could not help but admire the sultry curves on her tall, statuesque frame, it was her pretty face, the pert, straight nose and soft, sensual lips that had haunted his dreams.

One more night together shouldn't have made all the difference.

But it had.

Perhaps that's why it bothered him more than usual that

she'd been steadily avoiding his calls, texts and emails for the past six weeks, as was always the case after they hooked up....

His gut clenching with a mixture of impatience and anticipation, he watched Ginger stride toward him, her long legs eating up the ground. Slender shoulders squared, her chin held high, she moved with a smooth, effortless grace that made his heart jackhammer in his chest. Unfortunately there was no way of telling what she was thinking or feeling, given the sunglasses shading her dark green eyes. Figuring it best that he be standing when they faced off, Rand straightened to his full height. He set the soil sample in the bed of his truck. Inched off his leather gloves. Waited.

Her purposeful steps stopped just in front of him. Keenly aware that she owed him a big apology, for her usual lack of post-hooking-up etiquette, he looked at her expectantly.

Several long moments passed. Then she stuck her hands in the back pockets of her jeans and squared her shoulders again. Another beat of silence. Finally she said, "There's no other way to put this, so I'm just going to spit it out. I'm pregnant."

Pregnant. The word rolled around in his brain, refusing to compute. She was pregnant?

Ginger offered a weak smile, but did not take off her sunglasses. The silence between them stretched. Within him, anger and irritation surged. *After weeks of ignoring him, now this?* He took off his sunglasses, so she *could* see *his* eyes.

"Is this an April Fool's joke?" he demanded. Yet another way to torment him? If so, he wasn't laughing.

Every inch of her five-foot-eight-inch frame tensed. She let out a long, slow breath that first lifted then lowered her full shapely breasts. "Believe me, McCabe, I was as caught off-guard as you are."

He stared at her, still considering what to do and say next that wouldn't make the situation even more volatile.

Finally she took off her sunglasses.

To his surprise, she looked calm. Every emotional defense she had firmly in place. As though this whole speech was something she had rehearsed.

"Anyway." Ginger paused, appearing not to share the complex feelings roiling around inside him. "I thought I should tell you. Probably in person." She took another deep breath, suddenly looking oddly vulnerable. "So..." She gestured broadly, then started to pivot away from him.

Not about to let her run away from him again, especially now, he stopped her exodus with a light hand to her shoulder. Turned her slowly back to face him. "You're sure?" he asked quietly, searching her eyes, aware a sort of happy acceptance was beginning to crowd out the shock within him.

"Yes," she said softly, meeting his gaze for one long, telling moment that had them both—however briefly—on the same page. "When I first saw the plus sign in the indicator window, I was hoping it was a glitch in the home pregnancy test. Which is why—" She rummaged around in her back pocket, finally producing a folded piece of paper. "I saw a doctor over in Marfa and had a blood test and physical exam."

Her fingers brushed his briefly as she gave him the paper. It had her name and confidential patient information, all right, as well as lab results and the word "Positive." Under diagnosis, he saw "Pregnancy" listed, along with a projected due date of November sixth.

Their eyes met once again. Emotion shimmered between them as another long, awkward silence fell. He wasn't sure what she expected of him. Wasn't entirely sure what he felt, either. Except for the tiny hint of joy.

She assessed him with a long, level look and blurted, "Aren't you going to ask me if the baby is yours?"

Rand knew that would have been the logical response if their latest one-night stand had been with two people who were accustomed to having one-night stands. Neither of them was. That made her habitual running away from him—from the passion they shared—all the harder to understand and accept, given that their intermittent lovemaking had been ongoing for more than a year now.

"No."

Her green eyes glimmered with barely suppressed emotion. "Why not?"

"Because I don't have to, Ginger," he said. "I *know* it is."

Seeming vaguely insulted by his confidence, she squinted at him, then retorted, "How?"

Aggravated to find her still wanting to downplay what they'd experienced, which had been pretty spectacular, he returned, just as contentiously, "Because it was apparent from the very first time we ever went to bed together that you knew nothing about having a fling, and even less about turning an ongoing *series of flings* into a relationship."

She flushed. Guilty as charged. Shaking her head, she rasped, "We are such a bad match."

In certain ways, Rand conceded readily. In others... He couldn't disagree more. Because deep down, he had never felt anything like what he felt when he was with her. Nor—if his instincts were correct—had she. She was just too stubborn to admit it.

Sensing she was about ready to bolt, he let out a rough breath and stepped closer. "Well, given that we have a little one on the way, we're going to have to find a way to do better."

His gruff reminder brought a much needed dose of reality back to the situation.

"I agree," Ginger said. "Which is why," she continued resolutely, looking straight at him, "I'd like the two of us to make it official, at least for a while."

FOR ONCE, Ginger noted, Rand McCabe had absolutely nothing to say. And that left her scrambling to put a halt to whatever confused notions he had. Hating how awkward this all felt, she lifted a cautioning hand. "Naturally, it won't be a real relationship."

Something flickered in his blue eyes then fled. "Naturally."

Trying not to think how attracted to him she was, she cleared her throat. "It'd be more like a business arrangement to get us through the birth."

And since they were both small business owners, she figured he would appreciate her matter-of-fact approach to their predicament. To her shock, however, it seemed to have done the opposite.

Still trying to get some sense of where she stood with him, Ginger let out a shaky breath and added, "Although there are obvious social advantages to being a 'family' while we await the birth of our baby…legally, it would also be easier."

He lifted a questioning brow, his gaze roving her head to toe.

Tingling everywhere his eyes had touched—and everywhere they hadn't—Ginger explained, "Under Texas law, a child born to a man and woman who are not married has no legal father. Conversely, if we're husband and wife when the baby is born, the child will automatically be yours in the eyes of the law. No additional paperwork will need to be done to establish paternity before we can put your name on our child's birth certificate."

"Looks like you've thought of everything," Rand said dryly.

Ginger had certainly tried. "It's all online. You can research it through the Texas attorney general's website, too."

Again, Rand merely nodded.

Frustrated he wasn't more forthcoming with his thoughts and feelings, she groaned. "Fortunately, we won't have to stay married too long." A little less than nine months, the way she figured it.

This time he moved closer. He stopped mere inches short of her. She inhaled the scent of soap and sun and man.

His blue eyes gleamed. "So you're proposing to me?"

Why did she suddenly feel as though that was a bad thing? "I know that's typically a man's domain."

He lowered his head, until they were nose to nose and she had no choice but to look into his eyes. "Uh, yeah!"

His gruff words were a direct hit to her carefully constructed defenses. Aware there were times when he made her feel very safe, and times—like now—when he made her feel very off-kilter, Ginger shrugged nonchalantly. "But I didn't want to wait for you to get around to it."

He smiled. "You think I'd take my sweet time about it, is that it?"

He certainly took his sweet time about a lot of things. In bed, anyway. Ginger flushed, disturbed that the only way they knew each other all that well, was sensually.

She waved off his assertion. "Don't know. Don't care." She moved to put her sunglasses back on, but stuffed them in her vest pocket instead. "I just want a ring on my finger before any more time elapses. So that by the time I'm showing and we have to start telling people I'm pregnant, we'll already be married, and it won't be such a big deal."

His eyes never left hers as he stood there in that utterly disarming way that he had. "Oh, it's a big deal, all right," he said in a low, soft voice that sent ribbons of sensation coasting down her spine.

She craned her neck to meet his gaze. "You know what I mean, McCabe. If we've already been hitched for three months or so before I have to start telling people I'm expecting, then people aren't going to think much of it. It's going to be old news a lot faster than it otherwise would be."

"Or in other words—" his eyes never wavered from her face "—you don't want people to think we *had* to get married."

Determined to keep him at arm's length, Ginger fought the waves of sexual magnetism that always existed between them. "There's no such thing as having to get married in this day and age. But…"

He frowned. "There's always a caveat with you, isn't there?"

So what if there is? Ginger liked to be prepared for any eventuality, especially the bad stuff.

She stiffened her spine and plunged on. "Since the majority of the clients I want to put under contract are very traditional in their outlook, it makes sense for me—us—to be married. So that I will appear more…"

"Settled?"

She gave him a withering look before finally conceding, "Traditional, too."

Rand rubbed the flat of his palm across the nape of his neck. "Except for the fact that anyone who knows you at all kind of knows that you aren't conventional, Ginger. Not in the slightest."

True, she hadn't been. Until she'd realized they had a baby on the way. Knowing she had to provide for someone other than herself had changed everything. Made her yearn for as much stability as possible in her personal—and professional—life. Which included finding a way to land her first big contract as an independent oil woman, ASAP.

"Marrying you will show everyone that I'm finally ready to settle down. That it's safe to trust my skill as a geologist, and to sign with me."

And that, in turn, would give their child the safe harbor he or she would need, even after she and Rand parted ways.

He sighed. "So this isn't just about the baby. It's about oil, too?"

Ginger nodded, as ready to be totally upfront about that as everything else. "The word on the street is that Summit County is going to lift their temporary moratorium on horizontal drilling any day now. When that happens, there's going to be a stampede of wildcatters trying to get landowners signed up."

"In particular Dot and Clancy Boerne."

A brief smile flickered across her face. "The fifty-thousand-acre Boerne ranch is where the most oil is expected to be."

"You think being pregnant and unmarried would eliminate you from the running?" he asked, sliding her a long, contemplative look.

In a word, yes. Ginger shrugged. "It's no secret that I've had an uphill battle trying to convince people to do business with me because I'm young, and female and a lot less experienced than some of the others vying for business."

He grinned, as if admiring her moxie. "And yet you persist."

He was darned right she did. "Just because wildcatting is still primarily a man's domain, doesn't mean it needs to stay that way."

Rand spoke with the respect of a son of the best lady

wildcatter in the state of Texas, Josie Corbett-Wyatt Mc-Cabe. "Of course not."

"Furthermore, I've already demonstrated time after time I have a knack for coming up with drilling plans that get oil out of places that were previously considered inaccessible." Drilling plans that should have had her promoted at her previous job with Profitt Oil, if there had been any fairness involved. Which there hadn't been. "I just need a chance to show everyone what I can do now that I've ventured out on my own."

He rubbed the flat of his hand beneath his jaw. "Well, as long as you're confident…"

"I didn't expect you to cheer me on. Since all you want to do is *stop* people from drilling—"

"Irresponsibly," he interrupted, adding that important qualification. He had nothing against getting oil out of the ground, as long as it was done safely and with minimal environmental impact.

Ginger planted her hands on her hips, aware they were on the verge of yet another of their famously passionate arguments. "Well, I'm *not* irresponsible."

"And yet you're pregnant."

Ginger flushed. She should have known he would bring the conversation back to their lovemaking. He always did when they clashed, probably because he knew the topic got her even more worked up. "You get half the credit for that, cowboy. And it's not as though we didn't…"

"Use protection?" A hint of amusement filled his voice.

Ginger shook her head. "If the condom hadn't broken that one time…"

"There'd be no baby on the way."

No reason for them to be together now.

Another silence fell, this one slightly less combative.

Aware that if she wasn't careful she really would fall

under his spell, Ginger stepped back and turned away. Needing a moment to pull herself together again, she swept off her hat and ran her fingers through her hair, doing her best to restore order to the tousled strands. For a long moment her gaze traversed the winding creek, fields of wildflowers and the granite mountains rising in the distance. With the blue sky overhead, and a warm breeze flowing over them, it really was a beautiful spring day. Quiet, too, since the Trans-Pecos region of far west Texas was not just rugged and vast, but sparsely populated.

But that, too, would change if what everyone was predicting, the oil boom that had already hit many other areas of the state, actually happened here in Summit County.

With a sigh, Ginger turned back to Rand. Realized all over again just how devastatingly handsome he was. As she finally met his eyes, she sensed she wasn't the only one feeling conflicted about everything that was going on. "Look. I know it goes against your grain, having to get hitched to me, even temporarily. That when the time comes for you to really settle down, you'll want someone a lot more…more…" She grasped for the right word.

He leaned forward and helped her out. "Demure?"

Irked, she narrowed her eyes at him and slapped her hat back on her head. "Whatever." Although to be truthful she couldn't imagine him with anyone else. "As far as you and I are concerned, however, this is only a temporary arrangement. One that can be undone as soon after the baby is born as possible."

"And in the meantime?"

Ginger shrugged. "We don't even have to live together. Well, not really," she added hastily. "Especially if you end up working in another part of the state—"

"Not happening. I'm consulting in Summit County until the boom is over, same as you."

She had been afraid of that. "Then we'll get a place with separate bedrooms."

"Why?" He smirked in a way meant to infuriate. "We'll only end up in the same one."

"No. We. Won't. Sleeping together is what got us into this mess."

He rubbed his jaw with maddening nonchalance. "Keep dreaming, sweetheart." The corner of his mouth twitched in barely checked amusement. "That's one vow you'll never keep."

Flustered by his blatant delight at her frustration, Ginger shoved her hand through her hair. She didn't know why she let him get to her this way. "I don't know what it is about you and me that has us arguing every time we're around each other," she complained.

The wicked gleam in his eyes said *he* did.

"But right now," Ginger continued single-mindedly, "we need to focus on the least disruptive and most expedient way to say our I Do's."

Rand looked no more eager to head home and involve their families than she did. "Right here in Summit County is fine with me."

"Me, too," Ginger breathed, glad they were finally in concert about something. But then she felt the compelling pull of his gaze and her relief fizzled away. Steadfastly ignoring the shimmer of awareness sifting through her, she went back to her truck to collect the research she had already gathered, in preparation. Returning, she handed him his copy. "So here's the plan…."

RAND HAD NEVER been one to let a woman take the lead. It just wasn't in his nature. However, he knew that Ginger was right; they needed to get married as quickly as possible. Otherwise, Ginger was likely to change her mind and bolt again. Only this time she'd be taking his unborn child with her.

So the two of them left the creek bed and went straight to the county clerk's office in Summit, Texas. They applied for a marriage license and made an appointment with a justice of the peace for as soon as the three-day waiting period expired.

"So I'll see you here Thursday at noon?" Ginger said on the courthouse steps after they had finished the paperwork.

Rand nodded. "You want to meet here? Or have me pick you up?"

"We can meet here."

He had figured she would say that. Although that, too, was going to have to change. Married people rode in the same vehicle, at least from time to time.

Pausing again, Ginger eyed him cautiously. "I'm just going to wear jeans…"

He shrugged. What did it matter since this wasn't a real marriage? "Okay."

"So no tie or anything," Ginger persisted.

He hooked his thumbs through the loops on either side of his fly. "Shirt and shoes optional, too?"

Flushing slightly, she told him archly, "You know what I mean."

He sure did. He rocked forward on his toes. "How about flowers? You want a corsage or anything?"

"Certainly not!" She appeared insulted at the thought.

He lowered his face until they were nose to nose. "You're bringing your own?"

She scoffed in disgust and stepped back in a drift of orange blossom perfume. "I'm not having any."

Of course she wasn't. Aware Ginger brought the *D* to *difficult,* Rand retorted, "Is everything about us—as a couple—going to be this nonsensical?"

"Ultra casual," she corrected. "And probably."

Rand could only imagine how their families were going to take to that. His parents didn't necessarily want everything to be fancy, but they did expect occasions such as weddings to be incredibly special. He'd only met Ginger's mother once—in passing—but Cordelia Rollins had struck him as the ultimate helicopter parent. And one who would definitely want a big elaborate wedding for her only daughter. *Not* a hasty elopement.

"All right, then," Rand said finally, making note not to adorn his new bride with any gift of a sentimental nature. "Good to know."

Ginger's hands flew to her hips. "You don't have to be so caustic."

As if he had started it. He let his gaze drift lazily over her before returning to her beautiful, emerald eyes. "You don't have to be so prickly," he shot back.

Her chin lifted in that all-too-familiar way. She sized him up for a long, thoughtful moment, then stepped a little closer. "Well, maybe it's a good thing you're so impossible."

He shortened the distance between them even more, until only mere inches remained, then drawled, "And why, pray tell, is that?"

"Because then it won't be a surprise to anyone when we decide to go our separate ways a year from now."

"Or sooner," he allowed with a sigh, not seeing at that moment how they were going to make it one month as a married couple, much less all the way to their baby's birth.

"So…I'll see you Thursday?" she said finally.

He held her gaze, aware that for reasons he preferred not to examine *too* closely, he was looking forward to their next step every bit as much as *she* seemed to be openly dreading it. "At noon."

Her mouth twitching with satisfaction, she decreed, "I'll see you then," and sashayed off toward her pickup without a backward glance.

Chapter Two

True to her word, Ginger showed up on the courthouse steps Thursday at noon. In worn jeans, fancy Western boots, a white, lace-trimmed knit shirt and rose-colored vest, she looked pretty as a picture. "Ready?" she asked.

"As I'll ever be," Rand returned, more than ready to get the formality over with, too.

They walked into the courthouse, side by side. Only to promptly discover, to their mutual dismay, that all was not as it should be, after all.

"What do you mean we can't get married today?" Ginger lamented when they found out the justice of the peace set to conduct their ceremony was not even on the premises. "We made an appointment to get married at noon!"

"I know." The middle-aged court clerk swept a hand over his buzz-cut hair. "And believe me, the justice is sorry, but it can't be helped. It's a 'family' thing." Then he continued, a little lamely, "So if you all want the J.P. to marry you, you're going to have to reschedule…"

Not about to give up that easily, Rand asked, "Is there someone else who could perform the ceremony?"

"Not today. But…" The clerk studied the calendar on the computer in front of him. "The J.P. could fit you in a week from now, at three."

A week was too long to wait. Rand could see his bride-to-be thought so, too.

Ginger swung toward him, her body nudging his in the process. "What are we going to do?" she asked plaintively. "You told your parents you're coming to Laramie this evening to see them." She threw up her hands. "My mother is expecting me in San Angelo first thing tomorrow morning."

They hadn't told either of their families they weren't coming alone. That news, they had figured, could wait until they arrived, announced their "elopement" and introduced their new spouse, all in one fell swoop.

Aware she was sounding a little more emotional than usual—probably due to her pregnancy—Rand felt a surge of protectiveness rush through him. He gave Ginger's hand a brief, reassuring squeeze. "And we'll keep those promises," he said.

He dropped her hand and turned back to the clerk with a possible solution. "Do we have to get married in Summit County for our license to be valid?"

The beleaguered clerk perked up. "No, sir. Anywhere in the State of Texas is fine."

Rand thanked the clerk and they left the justice of the peace's office.

Ginger shot Rand a sidelong glance as they walked toward the exit. Their footsteps echoed on the polished marble floors. "I gather you have a plan?" she asked.

"I do." He held the door for her, and accompanied her out into the midday heat of the spring day and down the broad limestone steps. "Even better, the place is sort of a McCabe family tradition. Which means—" he paused to give her a level look, hoping she would cooperate with him just this once "—it'll give our union an air of authenticity we probably wouldn't get any other way."

Although they hadn't talked about it, Ginger seemed to know what a hard sell their surprise elopement was going to be—for both families. Their eyes met and held once again. After a moment she took a deep breath, squared her slender shoulders and vowed softly, "Then I'm all-in."

AT RAND'S INSISTENCE, they would leave her truck behind and take his pickup for the drive north.

At Ginger's insistence, they phoned ahead to their destination, to make sure that Jeff-Paul Randall could marry them. The internet-certified minister slash business owner promised to be there when they arrived around five o'clock.

Relieved to have that arranged, Ginger climbed into the passenger seat of Rand's gray hybrid pickup and settled in beside the tall, broad-shouldered Texan.

Trying not to think about the fact he would soon be her husband, at least in name only, Ginger turned her attention to the rugged scenery. The creosote flats peppered with yucca and cholla cactus gradually gave way to elevations of higher rainfall, pinyon pine and scrub oak. Oil wells, cattle ranches and the occasional wind farm abounded, but towns were few and far between as they traversed the canyons, landed on Interstate 20 and gradually left the desert prairies and majestic mountains of the Trans-Pecos behind.

Rand said little during the four-and-a-half-hour drive. Ginger was quiet, too. In truth, there wasn't much to say. She just wanted the elopement to be over and done with. Although he didn't say as much, she was pretty sure Rand felt that way, too.

Finally they hit the outskirts of Laramie County. Minutes later they approached their destination: J.P. Randall's Bait and Tackle Shop. The squat, flat-roofed building with its peeling white paint was in the middle of nowhere, and just rundown enough to make it disreputable without being dangerous. Frequented by sportsmen and campers en route to Lake Laramie from the west, as well as people looking to fill up their gas tanks, or to be wed in a hurry, it was usually populated by a few cars and trucks.

Ginger knew, because she had stopped there herself a few times when in this part of the state. Never before, though, had she seen the establishment rimmed by three Laramie County Sheriff's Department squad cars. "I wonder what's going on."

Rand frowned. "The lights aren't flashing on the squad cars. Nothing is cordoned off by yellow tape…"

When Rand shrugged his broad shoulders, Ginger hitched in a breath. Masculine sinew strained against the soft chambray of his shirt, and she yearned to feel those smooth, rippled muscles beneath her fingertips.…

"Maybe the deputies are just on a break," he said, snapping her out of her reverie.

"Maybe." Still, her feminine intuition told her it was more than that.

His expression serious, Rand pulled into the lot. The two of them got out of his pickup just as three men in khaki uniforms exited the shop. They grinned in recognition and Rand muttered a low curse as one of the men raised a hand in greeting. The other two deputies amiably followed suit.

Ginger pivoted to her husband-to-be.

So much for relative secrecy, she thought. "Obviously you know these men," she drawled. No surprise, in a rural county, where he had not only been born, but grown up.

Rand locked eyes on the approaching trio of law enforcement officers. A half smile tugged at the corners of his lips, yet his gaze remained wary. "Yep."

Her body tingling with a mixture of frustration and wariness, Ginger turned her attention back to the trio. All were about Rand's age, which meant early- to mid-thirties.

All were well over six feet tall with fit, muscular physiques, all teemed with testosterone. But one of them was more similar to Rand than the other two. The badge on his chest said Deputy Colt McCabe.

It was all Ginger could do not to groan. "Tell me you're not related."

"Okay, we're not related," Rand repeated facetiously.

Except they clearly were.

Deputy Colt McCabe slapped Rand on the back. "Hey, there, baby brother."

Rand braced, as if ready for more teasing. "Colt." The word was clipped and dry, yet oddly welcoming.

Colt McCabe's wicked smile broadened. He inclined his fine-looking head at Ginger and asked his brother, "Aren't you going to introduce us to your friend?"

Keeping his gaze trained on his older brother's, Rand angled his thumb at Ginger, as if they were no more than the most casual of acquaintances. A fact that for some unknown reason annoyed the heck out of her.

"This is Ginger Rollins." He turned, briefly catching her eye. Warning flashed in his expression. He, too, thought something was up, and wordlessly urged her to play along with whatever he said and did.

And really, Ginger thought, what choice did she have?

"Ginger," Rand continued with laudable politeness, "my brother Colt."

Colt tipped his Stetson in her direction. "Pleased to meet you."

Rand went on reluctantly. "This is Rio Vasquez." He nodded at the olive-skinned lawman, then the dark-haired man beside him. "And my cousin, Kyle McCabe."

Ginger shook all three deputies' hands in turn and uttered a cheerful greeting to each.

"So what brings the two of you to the bait shop?" Colt asked.

Ginger had a feeling, from the way Colt McCabe's eyes had initially been twinkling, that he already knew. So much for their plan of calling ahead to ensure there were no further delays.

Rand kept his poker face. "Nothing much," he told his older brother. "You?"

Colt's silence was answer enough.

Rio continued, in all seriousness, "We heard you have a marriage license in your possession that was issued in Summit County four days ago."

Rand pressed his fingers to his eyes and grimaced.

Wondering what her husband-to-be knew that she didn't, Ginger asked, "Is there a problem?"

All three deputies exchanged looks. "Mind if we take a look at it?" Kyle McCabe asked.

Unhappy that their marriage license might somehow be suspect, Ginger took it out of her handbag and handed it over. Kyle inspected it, then showed it to Vasquez and McCabe. All three shook their heads in silent remonstration.

"Just as we thought," Rio declared, eyes twinkling.

Kyle McCabe handed the license back to Ginger and said, "We're going to need the two of you to get back in your vehicle and follow us."

Whatever the joke, Rand was clearly not in the mood. He paused, as if weighing his options. "And if we don't?" he challenged.

Colt McCabe gave his younger brother another long, provoking look. "I think you can imagine," he retorted. "Sometimes it's just best to go along to get along, if you know what I mean."

"Go along with *what?*" Ginger asked.

Rand shoved a hand through his mahogany hair and

muttered something under his breath that Ginger was just as glad not to be able to decipher. More meaning-laced looks passed between the four men.

Aware Rand seemed more exasperated and annoyed than concerned about whatever it was that was going on, Ginger knit her brow in consternation. "Is there something wrong with the marriage license?" Because if there was…

More looks. These seeming to tell Rand to keep her in the dark, at least for a little while longer.

Rand placed a protective hand at her back and turned Ginger toward his truck. He leaned down, his warm breath brushing her ear and muttered, "We only wish that were all this was."

"YOU WANT TO tell me what's really going on?" Ginger asked when the caravan had headed down the highway, in the opposite direction from which they'd come.

A mixture of resentment and resignation warred on his handsome face. "I'd rather not speculate," he said finally.

Okay. Next question. "Do we even have to go with them, then?" The three lawmen had made it clear, as they were getting in their patrol cars, that they weren't currently "on duty" with the sheriff's department. Colt had just gotten off shift, Rio hadn't yet started his and Kyle was on break. So, it was clear that whatever this was, it wasn't exactly official.

"No," Rand returned in a low voice. Having come to terms with their predicament, though, he was resigned to handling it with his usual good humor. "But we'd just be putting off until later what we may as well handle now."

Ginger rolled her eyes. "Well, that clears things up."

Rand reached over, put his hand on her knee and gave it a friendly squeeze. "Want my advice?"

Making no effort to hide her growing frustration, she

plucked his hand from her leg as if it were an odious insect. "No, but I guess you're going to give it to me anyway."

Rand chuckled. "I suggest you relax and enjoy the peace and quiet, because it sure as heck won't last for long."

Turned out, Rand was right about that. The minute they passed beneath the wrought-iron archway announcing the spread owned by Wade and Josie McCabe, and headed down the tree-lined path to the big stone-and-cedar ranch house, they saw the catering trucks and the big white tents on the back lawn. Musicians were already setting up. Acutely aware of their casual attire, Ginger shot Rand a startled look. "Please tell me your parents are having a party."

"It would appear so."

She added the important caveat, "One that *doesn't* involve us."

"That, I can't say one way or another. I can tell you all four of my brothers are already here. As well as…"

Ginger's face fell. She recognized the white Cadillac sedan with the vanity plate #1TXMOM. Her hand flew to her throat. "Oh, no. My mother." A litany of frustrated words followed.

Rand mirrored her feelings with a groan of his own as the front door to the ranch house swung open and a bevy of McCabes and Rollinses poured out.

Ginger's mother was dressed in a beaded knee-length suit suitable for a mother of the bride. Perhaps because they were the ones throwing the bash, Josie and Wade were still in jeans, boots and loose-fitting cotton shirts. All three parents looked as privately exasperated and publicly determined as Rand and Ginger felt.

Rand and Ginger got out of the pickup, waved goodbye to the departing lawmen and met their families midyard. "How did you find out?" Rand asked.

Josie McCabe scowled at her youngest son. "A reporter from the *Summit Journal-News* called me three days ago to ask me how I felt about my environmentalist son marrying a rival lady wildcatter. From there it was easy enough to find out a marriage license had been issued, so I called Cordelia Rollins to find out what she knew…"

Ginger's mom picked up where Josie left off. "And lo and behold, I knew nothing."

Wade added, "We all talked and decided if you two were going to get married, you were going to do it with friends and family present."

Josie nodded. "So I called the justice of the peace in Summit and asked him to hold off."

That explained the mysterious family matter that had kept the court official from marrying Rand and Ginger. "We already knew you were coming home this evening, so it was…well, not easy—" Josie frowned "—but possible, with Cordelia's help, to get a wedding set up here."

Rand quirked a brow. "What if we had canceled our trip north this evening?"

Josie shrugged. "I would have invented an emergency to get you here anyway."

"And what if we were already married when we got here?" Ginger asked her mother.

"Then you would have been married again, by a proper minister, in proper wedding clothes," Cordelia replied, shaking her head in reproach. "Honestly, Ginger, you are my only daughter. Were you really going to deny me the chance to see you pledge your love to the man of your dreams? Even if I haven't yet had the opportunity to even meet him, never mind give my blessing!"

If there was anything Ginger hated more than interference in her personal life, it was melodrama. "Well, as long as you put it that way," she quipped, raking a hand through her hair.

"You, too, young man," Josie scolded, stomping closer. "You know better!"

To Ginger's relief, she wasn't the only one taking exception to their public dressing down.

"Look," Rand was saying to his mother, "it's not as if I haven't done this once before. I had a proper wedding the first time around."

Rand had been married before? To whom? Ginger wondered, a tinge of jealousy trickling through her. But there was no time to delve into it. She could see that both mothers expected her, at least, to want the big, ultra-romantic wedding they had painstakingly organized, in lieu of the quick, no-frills elopement she and Rand had been hoping to have. Hence, Ginger had no choice but to set the record straight.

She sighed in exasperation. "I also had a big fancy wedding the first time." A fact her mother well knew. Consequently there was no need to go through that circus again. Even if the union she and Rand were planning had been a real marriage, which it wasn't.

Both mothers seemed stunned by the twin revelations.

Rand and Ginger turned to look at each other. Belatedly she realized she didn't know much about Rand, except how he felt about the environment and how great he was in bed. He knew very little about her, as well.

Abruptly aware they had overlooked a very important part of the marriage process, Ginger looked at Rand. "I think I need a moment alone with my, uh, fiancé."

"Good idea." Rand took Ginger by the arm and they headed down the driveway, not stopping until they were well out of earshot of everyone. Pivoting so no one would be able to read her lips, Ginger said ruefully, "We probably should have written a prenup."

LEAVE IT TO Ginger, Rand thought, taking in her soft, kissable lips and too vulnerable green eyes, to bring a highly emotional situation right back to cold, hard business. It was something she always did when she felt backed into a corner in any way. Something, in the end, that always drove him away.

Not this time. Not when she was carrying their child.

Aware all eyes were still likely upon them, Rand shrugged. "No time to do it tonight."

Ginger blinked up at him and raked her teeth across her lower lip. A pulse worked in her throat. "But we'll draw something up first chance we get?"

Rand nodded. As much as he would have preferred not to have to put themselves through that, Ginger had a point. It would make things simpler in the long run, if they put everything in writing well in advance of their divorce.

"In the meantime," Ginger continued practically, "in lieu of an actual marriage contract…how about a handshake deal?"

Cocking his head, he studied her face. "I'm listening."

"What's mine is mine, and what's yours is yours. There will be no community property gained during the union for us to quarrel about."

Her voice was calm enough, but he heard the steel-magnolia undertone. There would be no negotiating this or anything else in their union, at least as far as she was concerned.

He had a different idea.

Because he wasn't about to be pushed around by Ginger or any one else. "Everything regarding custody of our child will be equal, too."

This time she did not hesitate. "Right."

He relaxed in relief. "Okay, then." He tugged her in close and put one arm around her waist, shaking her other hand surreptitiously, in the age-old sign of a satisfactorily completed business deal. He whispered against her temple, "Let's do it."

"All right, you two!" Cordelia called from behind them. "Enough of that! We've got a wedding to put on!"

Once again, family interfered. Rand was escorted one way, Ginger another. A flurry of preparations followed.

Two hours later they were all together again, surrounded by two hundred of their closest family and friends.

This wasn't supposed to be anything more than a temporary legal formality, Rand thought in surprise. But standing next to the flower-strewn arbor in his parents' backyard, with a string quartet playing and his brother Colt stepping in to serve as best man, it sure felt like a real wedding. And, if the sweetly vulnerable look on Ginger's face as she floated down the aisle on her mother's arm was any indication, she was completely taken aback by the unexpected authenticity of the moment, too.

Colt teased Rand affectionately as Ginger neared. "I understand why you were in such a hurry to get a ring on her finger."

Ginger *was* beautiful, Rand thought, taking the opportunity to drink her in. Never more so than right now in her wedding finery.

The ivory-satin gown lovingly cupped her breasts, nipped in at her waist and left her arms and shoulders bare. The full skirt fell in a seductive swirl past her ankles. A sparkling tiara, attached to a short veil, was threaded through her upswept copper hair. As she neared him, her eyes met his. Held. As he took her hand in his, her delicate cheeks grew pink and her soft lips parted. Her chest rose as she took in a deep, enervating breath.

And then the ceremony began.

GINGER HADN'T BEEN this caught up in the ceremony the first time she'd been to the altar. To be feeling so breathless with excitement was…well, completely unprecedented, unexpected. And, she forced herself to admit, unrealistic. Yet, standing there with her hands clasped in Rand's large, capable palms, looking deeply into his midnight-blue eyes, she couldn't help but feel a little swept away.

Maybe it was the way he looked in that dark tuxedo, the striking contrast of the stark white shirt against the suntanned hue of his skin. Or how closely he had shaved, and the way his mahogany hair shone in the evening light. All she knew was that he smelled so damn good, like a sundrenched forest just after a spring rain. That he felt so warm and was so tall and strong.

Maybe it was true, she thought, that women did instinctively search out the best specimen to father their children.

Right now, he seemed like the perfect mate.

To the point, it was easy to promise to have and to hold from this day forward.

At least, she added mentally, until the day their baby was born.

Then they'd see.

As she gazed into his eyes, she wondered if he was thinking the same thing.

That, too, would be reassuring. Because it would mean they might have all the trappings of a real marriage.

But "real" was, like this union, in the eye of the beholder.

The minister's voice rose, interrupting her thoughts. "What God has joined together, let no man put asunder." The reverend smiled broadly. "Rand, you may kiss your bride."

And heaven help them both, he did.

Chapter Three

But it wasn't just any generic end-of-the-wedding-ceremony-with-everybody-watching kind of kiss, Ginger thought in stunned amazement. It was a knock-your-shoes-off, make-you-tingle-from-head-to-toe embrace that weakened her knees. And had her surrendering to the warm, sure pressure of his mouth in a way she had never ever yielded before.

Not even to him. Not even during that fateful night when they'd made the baby she was carrying inside her.

This was something new. Something wonderful. Something suddenly and unexpectedly sanctioned.

And darn it all if Rand didn't take full advantage of the situation. Both arms wrapped around her, he brought her closer, until she was hanging on to him, soaking up everything about him—his strength, his scent, his warmth and tenderness. He was amazingly solid and real, so very masculine and persuasive. A low helpless sound escaped her throat, and Rand continued kissing her with the same quiet, unrelenting determination he channeled into everything that mattered to him. Until she mirrored his overwhelming need to make this mean more than it had. If only for this one moment in time. If only for the sake of their child…

Giving herself over to the marriage the way she had recklessly already given herself over to him, Ginger sighed again and curled her fingers into the fabric of his tuxedo jacket. Going up on tiptoe, she pressed hers breasts to the hardness of his chest and shifted her arms to his shoulders. His encircled her waist. And he brought her nearer still... claiming her as his woman, his wife. Just as she claimed him as her husband.

RAND HADN'T INTENDED to let the kiss take on a life of its own. Hadn't intended to turn Ginger—and himself—on to the degree that he had. Yet he couldn't say he was surprised. Whenever they were together, it was like putting a lit match to tinder. And that was something everyone who cared about them needed to see and understand. Because he knew if he and Ginger didn't want a heck of a lot of interference from family, needing—belatedly—to understand how and why they had come together in the first place, that they had some authenticating to do.

Problem was, he was beginning to want a whole lot more than a strictly-for-show kiss. He was beginning to want her alone. To want the hot, intense connection that blew all their impossible barriers away. But that couldn't happen right now, not with an audience surrounding them. It would have to wait until later. When they were alone. Celebrating their first official night together as man and wife.

Ginger moaned softly, trembling in his arms. Reluctantly, Rand lifted his head, looked into her misty green eyes and heard a cheer of approval from the guests.

His bride's acquiescence turned to a glare only he could see. Loving her display of fiery temper almost as much as her gorgeous copper hair, Rand grinned. He leaned forward, kissed her temple again and then held out his arm. She grasped it, just above the elbow, and motioned him down. She then whispered in his ear, "You're going to pay for that one."

Rand suspected he would.

He couldn't wait.

AN EXHAUSTING FEW hours later the reception neared an end. Rand still looked incredibly handsome in his tux. Physically, Ginger was holding up, too. Emotionally was another matter. The strain of pretending to be every bit as ecstatic as they were expected to be had worn what felt like an enormous hole in her heart.

If any of this were real…

But it wasn't, Ginger reminded herself sternly.

And that meant she and Rand had to get out of there before they got any more caught up in the festivities, and what it was all supposed to mean to them. Or would have, had any of this happened the traditional way.

Predictably, Rand read her mind as they finished feeding each other bites of scrumptious wedding cake. He kissed her temple and murmured in her ear, "Ready to make a run for it?"

Ginger tried not to let her inner weariness show. "More than you know," she whispered back.

Two of Rand's brothers appeared at their side. "Don't forget the garter removal and the bouquet toss," Colt said, clapping Rand on the shoulder.

"Actually—" Rand winked "—I'm keeping that part private."

Ginger flushed at the sexy implication. Colt shook his head at his younger brother, grinning from ear to ear. She blushed all the more and flashed her groom a humorously reproving look. Now she *really* owed him.

Rand paused to wipe a smear of vanilla butter-cream frosting from the corner of her mouth, then kissed her lips gently. Excitement warred with the anticipation that had been building all night.

Feelings like this, Ginger knew, could be trouble. Feelings like this were what had gotten them into this mess in the first place. Rand seemed to intuit this, too. Unlike her, however, he didn't seem to mind.

"One last surprise." All three parents approached them. Along with Cordelia Rollins, Josie and Wade McCabe turned and gestured to the stretch limousine in the drive. "We arranged for a last-minute honeymoon, too."

Cordelia, who liked everything to be perfect, confessed fretfully, "Unfortunately, due to the short notice, we could only book you one night in the bridal suite at Lake Laramie Lodge. But if you'd like to stay on in a regular room, that's been set up, too."

Ginger and Rand shook their heads in unison. "Sorry, y'all," she told them, "but we're going to have to head back to Summit tomorrow."

Rand nodded. "We both have a lot of work to do."

Their parents looked disappointed for the two of them, but not surprised. One bouquet toss and a spirited goodbye later, and Ginger and Rand were cozily ensconced in the back of the limo. The glass divider was up, to allow them maximum privacy.

Sighing wearily, Ginger let her head fall back against the seat and she closed her eyes. Rand clasped her hand in his. "You okay?" he asked.

Was she? Ginger still felt that odd, unexpected emptiness in her heart. Telling herself it was just a reaction to all that had happened, she replied, "Yes. Just tired."

"Then we'll get you out of that dress and straight into bed."

That had her opening her eyes, turning her head.

Rand looked sheepish. "You know what I mean," he said.

Ginger did. And for that, she was grateful.

Rand—like the rest of the McCabe men—could be exceedingly gallant. She knew that side of him would come in handy when their baby was born.

Upon arrival, Rand and Ginger were whisked straight to the spacious suite on the top floor of the lodge. The thousand-foot space sported a living area, majestic bedroom and large spa-style bath. A big box of chocolates and a bottle of champagne on ice sat waiting, along with a sumptuous repast of fruit, bread and cheese. All in all, it was much too romantic, way too decadent and private, for comfort.

Ginger wondered how she was going to spend an entire night here, alone with Rand, and not do exactly what they had in the past…succumb.

"Would you like me to open the champagne for you?" the bellman asked cheerfully after setting their overnight bags down.

Rand declined the offer, then tipped the bellman, who promptly congratulated them again and headed out. Once they were finally alone, Rand looked her over, taking in every inch of her. "What's wrong?"

How about nearly everything? Ginger thought. Then, trying a diversionary tactic, said, "Did you ever wonder why our parents threw us a big lavish wedding instead of trying to stop us?"

ACTUALLY, RAND HAD given that a thought or two in the previous eight hours. Aware that Ginger still looked better than any woman had a right to look after the day they'd had, he locked the door and moved further into the room. "My mom and dad know there's no dissuading me once I set my mind to something." He watched as Ginger attempted to work the tiara and veil out of her upswept hair. When it seemed she needed a hand, he stepped in to assist. While she stood stock-still, he found the pins and gently worked them free. Finished, he handed her the headdress. "What about your mom? Why was she so eager to see us get hitched?"

Ginger lifted her skirts, showing a flash of silk-clad ankle, and paused to toe off her high heels. Before Rand could help her, she eased off her satin garter, too, and dropped it onto the coffee table between them. Ignoring his look of comically exaggerated disappointment, she said, "My mom says her thirty-year marriage was the best thing that ever happened to her, and she wants me married to the love of my life, too."

Rand drank in the orange-blossom scent of her perfume. "How'd she feel about your divorce?"

Ginger sighed and went back to working the pins out of her hair. Finished, she ran her fingers through the silky copper mane and arranged the softly curling strands over her bare shoulders. "She wasn't pleased we were calling it quits. But she also knew Conrad and I weren't making each other happy. So in the end, she wanted what's best for me."

Ginger glided over to the bar, and poured herself a glass of ginger ale. "What about your parents?" She slanted him a curious look. "How did they feel about you getting divorced?"

Rand took off his bow tie, undid the first two buttons on his shirt and hooked his jacket onto the back of a chair. "I think they were relieved, given that it wasn't much of a marriage. It only lasted a month."

Ginger looked as if she thought his hasty divorce didn't bode well for the two of them, either. She sat on one end of the sofa and propped her stocking-clad feet on the table. "How come?"

Rand picked up the fruit plate and settled next to her on the sofa. He munched on a tart green grape.

"Turns out that Diandra expected access to my trust fund once the ring was on her finger."

Ginger leaned over and helped herself to a strawberry. "And you refused."

Rand turned to face her, balancing the plate on his bent knee. "That trust is my safety net, in case anything ever happens that leaves me unable to work." He draped his right arm along the back of the sofa. "I'm not going to live on it."

Ginger's brow furrowed. "Diandra didn't know that before you two said 'I Do'?"

Rand let out a mirthless laugh. "I had told her as much. She never thought I'd stick with it when we could have used it to live luxuriously. Anyway, as soon as she saw I was serious, she filed for divorce. When that didn't change my mind, she ended it for good."

Ginger made a soft sound he couldn't even begin to interpret. "How old were you?"

"Twenty-two."

Her eyes widened. "Wow."

"Yeah."

She tilted her head and took a longer look. "And since?"

Rand shrugged. "There's been my work, as an environmentalist. And you." She flushed in response. "So what about you?" He ate another grape. "How long were you married?"

She toyed with a wedge of peach and lifted it to her mouth. "Four years."

He watched her savor the juicy fruit. "What happened?"

She shrugged. "I realized Conrad was never going to take me seriously in a professional sense."

He sensed that was the least of it. Frustrated she wasn't being more forthcoming, he searched her eyes and pressed on. "You felt disrespected?"

"And then some. Plus…" She hesitated.

He waited.

She bit her lip. "I had the feeling deep down that something was missing between Conrad and me. Anyway, we split up two years ago. Got a quickie divorce. And all my mother's done since is try to talk me out of the oil business and into another marriage that will last."

Rand saw trouble ahead. "Uh-oh."

"Yeah." Ginger wrinkled her nose. "She won't be happy when this union ends in divorce, too, but that is a problem for another day. My task right now is to get some sleep, ASAP."

Rand couldn't argue that. She was pregnant, after all. It had been a very long day. "Need some help getting out of that dress?"

Looking lovelier than ever, she stood, pivoted and arched a delicate brow. "Really?"

"Hey." He lifted his hands in mock surrender. "Just offering."

"Mmm-hmm." Shaking her head, Ginger went over to the luggage stand and opened her overnight bag. Blinked, and blinked again. A litany of frustrated words followed.

"What?" Curious as to what had her so upset, Rand rose and sauntered over. Ginger held up a very sexy white negligee in one hand and a very feminine sundress, equally unlike her, in the other. Aside from that, and a handful of very brief satin-and-lace undies, another pair of shoes, an unopened package of pantyhose and a toiletries bag, there was nothing in the bag. Trying not to imagine what she would look like in all or none of the above, he quipped, "Not what you were expecting?"

"Obviously, someone—my mother, most likely—took out everything I had planned to wear tonight and tomorrow, and replaced it with all this."

Rand's grin turned into a hearty chuckle.

Blushing mightily, Ginger wagged a finger in his direction. "You laugh now. But this begs the question. What's in *your* overnight bag, cowboy?"

GINGER WATCHED AS a bemused Rand plucked out a pair of discrete black satin boxers, a razor, more cotton underwear, a starched button-down shirt, a pair of khakis and another pair of shoes.

"Who did yours?"

Rand pointed to the proper morning-after-the-wedding clothing. "Probably my mother." He caught sight of a gift bag stuck in a side pocket. The names of all four of his brothers were on the tag. "And then—" Rand groaned at the contents: a G-string with a big silver wedding bell on the front "—my siblings got into the act."

Next to that, was a big box of condoms.

Not, Ginger thought, that they would be needing those— even if she hadn't already been pregnant. She rolled her eyes. "Nice."

"Thoughtful," he agreed. Putting everything down but the provocative scrap of spandex, he asked, "Want me to try it on?"

Actually, yes, but that would lead to nothing but trouble. And they were in enough hot water as it was. So, instead, she gave him The Look.

Grin widening, he set it down. "I'm guessing that's a no."

He, however, did not look any the less discouraged. Trying not to think about what the mischievous light in his blue eyes portended, Ginger went back to studying the contents of her bag, then buried her face in her hands. "Well, now what are we going to do?" She had hoped to get two rooms somewhere and wear practical cotton pajamas to bed. Alone.

Beside her, Rand shook his head, looking just as distraught. "I don't know. We can't wear any of this." He shrugged helplessly. "We'll just have to go to bed naked."

Ha! As if he could rope her into that! After the incredibly romantic evening they'd had? Even if it hadn't been their doing. "Nope. We won't. You know why? Because—" she disappeared into the bathroom and emerged victoriously with two thick white spa robes "—we have these!"

Rand stroked his jaw, looking ruggedly handsome as ever. He leaned close. Inhaling the scent of him, she realized he still smelled amazing. His expression amused, as if he knew where her thoughts kept wandering, he quipped, "Naked under that is good, too."

Ginger huffed in indignation. "I won't be naked."

His mouth quirked but he held his silence.

"I'll still have on my underwear." She felt the need to rush on. "Maybe my stockings, too." Just for good measure. With him around, she needed every bit of clothing she could get.

When he still said nothing, she turned her gaze back to his. He stood, legs braced apart, hands propped on his waist. "Now what are you thinking?"

His gaze trailed lazily over her before returning ever so slowly to her face. "I'm imagining what kind of frilly, sexy undies you do have on under that dress."

Squirming with embarrassment, Ginger caught a glimpse of herself in the mirror and saw her cheeks were a deep rose pink. "Well, you'll never know." Determined to keep him at arm's length, both emotionally and physically, Ginger swept into the large bath and shut the door behind her.

Unfortunately, she soon found out, Rand's playful attitude was the least of her problems.

"AND HERE I thought you'd be down to your skivvies by now," Rand drawled when Ginger finally surrendered to the inevitable and opened the bathroom door. She swept into the suite, the skirt of her wedding gown rustling softly as she moved.

To her relief, he had done nothing more about undressing. And was, in fact, reclining on the king-size bed, hands clasped behind his head. His pleated white shirt was half unbuttoned. His cufflinks were off, the sleeves rolled up past his muscular forearms. He'd taken off his shoes, too.

Once again, his eyes caressed her. His gaze lingered on the cleavage spilling out of her fitted bodice, then drifted languidly over her waist, hips and thighs "You do look a mite skinnier now, though," he said after his long, slow perusal.

Wishing there was another option, Ginger moved toward him reluctantly. "It's because I took my petticoat off."

"Ah." Another pause and furrow of his dark brow. "What's a petticoat?"

"The froufrou thing that goes under my skirt to make it stand out. It's sort of like a half-slip for formal attire." She perched beside him on the bed, aware he hadn't moved a muscle. He looked turned on and frustrated.

She swallowed around the sudden dryness of her throat. "And you knew that, didn't you?"

One corner of his mouth lifted in a sensual smile. "I might not have. Only having brothers and all that."

Ginger recollected what she knew about the state's most famously successful lady wildcatter. "But your mom…"

"Was a debutante in Dallas before she met and married my dad."

"And still goes to a party or two?" Ginger prompted.

Rand nodded proudly. "She does. Although she prefers jeans and boots and an oil rig to any black tie affair."

Ginger wiggled her toes, which were still aching from the hours spent in beautiful, impractical high heels. "I can second that."

Rand remained where he was. "So. What's your problem?" He had all the predatory watchfulness of a man in hot pursuit.

"I can't seem to get out of this dress," Ginger admitted reluctantly.

He appeared to mull that over. "You could sleep in it."

True, but...the fitted bodice was so snug. Ginger wrinkled her nose. "It wouldn't be very comfortable."

His grin turned wicked. "Ready to get naked, then?"

Heavens, no! "I just want you to undo the back of my dress. Please."

Kindness mixed with desire. He laid a hand across his heart. "Well of course I'll do my husbandly duty."

Not about to inquire what else that might entail, Ginger turned and reluctantly offered him her back.

Her pulse pounded as he shifted to the edge of the mattress and sat behind her. His bent knee just barely brushed the curve of her buttock. The sensation was exquisitely erotic and sensual. Shivering, Ginger shifted away from him.

He said nothing. Did nothing. She shot him an aggravated look over her shoulder. "Well?"

He lifted his broad shoulders in an affable shrug. "I was waiting on you to come back to me again."

They were close enough—too close—as it was. They did not need to have actual physical contact to accomplish this. She sucked in a tremulous breath. "Is everything between us going to be this difficult?"

At her irritable demand, a laugh escaped him. "I don't know. Is it?"

Groaning, she flounced back another inch. "Just undress me!"

His chuckle was warm and sexy, as if she had just given him the opening he needed. Not about to be seduced into thinking this was anything but a temporary business arrangement, Ginger clarified hotly, "You know what I mean."

"I do." His hands brushed the skin between her shoulder blades. He struggled with the triple row of close-set hooks at the top of her zipper. One by one, they eventually gave way.

Maddeningly, the zipper did not follow.

"Now what?" Ginger asked, finding the sudden stillness as excruciatingly erotic as his tender touch. Desire blossomed deep inside her.

Rand slid a hand between the fabric and her skin, his touch kindling her overwrought senses even more. "I just want to make sure…"

That she was spontaneously combusting from the inside out? Well, she was! "Rand, come on. Just do it!"

"Well, I sure hope no one can overhear us." Rand's voice took on his best needling aw-shucks tone. "Who knows what people might be thinking, us being in the bridal suite and all?"

Ginger groaned again at his clowning around and buried her face in her hands. Rand was doing what he always did when things got too intense between them. He used the combination of their mutual chemistry and his good humor to get her to relax. The trouble was, she didn't want to relax. Didn't want to let her guard down with him for one red-hot second.

Just like that, the zipper on her wedding gown came down, easy as you please. Cool air assaulted her spine.

Behind her, Rand sucked in his breath. And went very still.

Silk organza bodice pressed tightly against her breasts, Ginger pivoted to face him. "Now what's the holdup—?" she started to say. Then stopped at the expression on his face. She knew that look. All too well.

"I was right," he said. His blue eyes darkened as if he were imagining what the front view of her lace-and-satin bustier, garter belt and tiny panties would be. "Those are some mighty fancy underthings you've got on."

And some very elemental feelings they were both having, Ginger noted. "I think we should stop here," she said softly. Before they felt even more really and truly married than they did at this moment. Rand nodded, as if agreeing that things were getting way too complicated, way too fast.

"Probably should," he stated gruffly. "But...how about just one kiss?" Pulling her to him, he dropped his head low. His lips hovered just above hers, tempting...seducing. "It is our wedding night, after all."

Chapter Four

Knowing it was crazy to even pretend any of this could ever work out, Ginger started to pull back. Only to be brought slowly closer. "One kiss," Rand repeated. "That's all I'm asking."

And all, Ginger thought, she was prepared to give. But when his lips fit over hers, all rational thought went right out of her head. She moaned at the soft, sweet heat. The touch of his tongue to hers sent her even further over the edge. Pulse pounding, body trembling with need, she wrapped her arms around his neck and shifted even closer. Emotions soaring, she nestled the softness of her breasts into the sinewy hardness of his chest.

One kiss melded into another. And another.

The next thing Ginger knew, he was pulling her to her feet. Pushing her unzipped gown down. A circle of ivory satin puddled at her feet.

He paused to take her in; his eyes roving the fullness of her breasts, the nip of her waist and the swell of her hips before sliding downward, along her thighs. Clasping her to him, he kissed her cheek, the line of her jaw, her throat. His lips toured the hollow of her collarbone. Then, straightening slowly, his gaze raked over her with startling possessiveness. Once again, he enveloped her with his warm strength, seeming at that moment to be fighting his own battle.

Tenderness emanated from him as first his fingertips and then his mouth caressed the uppermost curve of her breast. His other hand slid down her back to her hips, finding the delicate stretch of exposed skin between panty and garter belt. His breath was hot against her skin, the lazy ministrations of his mouth giving her a whole body shiver. She arched helplessly, wanting him, wanting this, so much. Feeling wild and wanton, she pressed her lips to his.

He held her face in his hands. "You are so beautiful."

When he kissed her and touched her like that, she felt beautiful, inside and out. Thrilling at his touch, eager to explore his body, too, she undid the remaining buttons and spread the edges of his shirt. His smooth skin was delineated with hard ridges of muscle. Beneath her questing fingers, she could feel the slow, fierce beating of his heart. The tantalizing traces of his aftershave mingled with the clean fragrance of soap and the more masculine scent unique to him. Needing, wanting, she tangled her fingers in his hair, shimmied up against him, closer yet. "You're breathtakingly gorgeous, too."

He laughed softly, his demeanor wickedly sensual, his eyes dark with desire. "I'm glad you think so," he murmured, "because at least for the time being, you're stuck with me."

That, she was, Ginger thought as he kissed her again, his lips warm and sure as his work-roughened palms slid over her, bypassing the barriers of satin and lace. Her nipples beaded against his palms. Lower still, moisture flowed. She trembled as he disrobed her, piece by tantalizing piece, kissing her slowly and seductively all the while.

Anxious for more, she undressed him, too. Kneading, stroking, caressing. And only when she was writhing with passion, did he lower her to the bed and stretch out beside her.

Ginger's eyes drifted shut as Rand parted her thighs and moved between them, creating ripples of yearning. She caught her breath as the sensations spread and pleasure flooded her in hot, irresistible waves, filling her with sensations unlike any she had ever known, and then there was no more holding back. He cupped her bottom and lifted her toward him, and took her slowly, sweetly.

Emotion overwhelming her, she wrapped her arms and legs around him, urging him on, taking him deeper and deeper. She gave him everything. He demanded more, as did she. And then there was nothing but the intense power of their connection that had them soaring, free, together, once again.

RAND FELT GINGER'S regret in the slight stiffening of her body, the way he always did as their passion ebbed and their breathing slowed. He wasn't surprised when she extricated herself and slipped from the bed.

The bathroom door shut softly behind her.

He lay there, listening to the water run, and then all fell silent. He supposed she was using the time to get herself together. He couldn't blame her. It had been one heck of a day, full of surprises. But in the end, they had achieved their goal, gotten married, and in the process, miraculously received the blessings of their families. Had this been a real marriage, they would have been over the moon with happiness.

But because this wasn't the usual union, they had to deal with that, and somehow find a way to make it all work.

Figuring she'd been hiding out long enough, Rand got out of bed, pulled on his boxer briefs and walked across the suite. He rapped on the door. "Ginger?"

No answer.

"You okay in there?"

Again, no answer.

Beginning to panic a little, he eased open the door. Ginger was wrapped in a thick white spa robe and seated on the plush stool. She had one arm on the marble vanity in front of her. Her head was nestled in the crook of her elbow and turned toward him. Her breathing was soft and even. As he neared her, he saw the tears dampening her cheeks.

He touched her shoulder. "Ginger…"

She shifted, sinking ever deeper into slumber, and mumbled something incoherent.

Whether she accepted it or not, she needed to be in bed. Rand said her name once more, and when she did not wake, lifted her in his arms. He carried her to the bed and put her gently down, then walked around to the other side and slid in beside her.

Clearly she had her regrets. Suddenly he did, too. But he gathered her close anyway and wrapped his arms around her.

"You're sure you want to do this today?" Rand asked the following afternoon.

They'd been on the go since early morning, managing not to talk about anything that had happened the day before, or how their wedding night had ended, at least for Ginger—in private tears and exhausted sleep. Rand, on the other hand, had lain awake most of the night, wondering how they were going to make this all work.

And not just in the public eye.

"I thought I'd made it clear that I do." Ginger's determination increased tenfold as his pickup approached Summit's historic downtown.

The four-and-a-half-hour drive from Lake Laramie to

the Trans-Pecos area of Texas had done nothing but energize her. "We need to get this postnuptial agreement done."

Rand noted the vulnerability she had showed the day before had all but disappeared. And although he respected her strength, he resented the emotional distance she put between them every chance she got. He tightened his grip on the steering wheel.

"Agreed."

"But?"

He kept his eyes on the Main Street traffic. "I think it could wait until next week. Especially since it's just a formality."

Ginger adjusted her sunglasses on the bridge of her nose. "I never put off to tomorrow what can be done today."

Wasn't that the truth? Rand thought, parking the truck.

The two of them entered the brick building that housed Michelle Anderson-Garner's law office. The family law attorney, a willowy blonde in her late thirties, was waiting for them.

She took a seat opposite them in the conference room, and handed each a stack of forms and a pen.

"For this postnuptial agreement to be honored under Texas law, there must first be a full and fair disclosure of property and other financial aspects of each of your estates," she began. "So, basically, I need a detailed list of every asset and every debt each of you has, as well as any you may have accrued together. We can even go over who gets custody of the family pet, if you have one."

"What about kids?" Rand asked.

"Children are not covered under a prenuptual or postnuptial. Those issues are decided in family court."

"Can other issues be included in the postnup?" Ginger queried.

Michelle paused. "Such as?"

"Rand and I have agreed to run our marriage like a business."

"Okay…"

Ginger sat forward. "So I—we—were thinking of drawing up either a contract or bylaws that would detail how we are going to handle everything else."

Since when? Rand wondered, taken aback.

"That way," Ginger continued, "we wouldn't have to fight about things unnecessarily. We would already know how and where we're going to live, and so on."

Like most lawyers, Michelle had a remarkable ability to maintain a poker face. But even this, Rand noted, seemed to throw her for a loop. Not that he could blame the attorney. He'd come here under the impression they were only going to talk about financials.

Oblivious to the stunned reactions of the others in the room, Ginger carried on. "To be truly effective, our marriage contract should cover who is going to cook, or do laundry. Or, maybe we each should be on our own for these types of mundane chores."

Deciding as long as Ginger insisted on micromanaging all this, he might as well get what he wanted, too, Rand interjected casually, "The bylaws or marriage contract should also cover where we live. How many nights and days we can be apart at one time—or not be apart, as the case may be." He flashed Ginger a satisfied grin as his next idea hit. "Since both our jobs require travel, maybe we should stipulate that we at least take jobs in the same county."

Ginger's brow furrowed. Clearly she hadn't expected him to speak much at this meeting, if at all.

"Obviously we still have some things to work out…" she said.

"Privately," Rand added curtly. "And yes, we do."

Her spine stiffening, Ginger turned back to Michelle.

"The point is, Rand and I have both already been divorced once. Neither relationship ended amicably, probably because we both went into those unions too naively. We're determined not to make the same mistake again." Ginger squared her shoulders. "Which is why we want to work all this out now."

Having absorbed everything his wife had said, the attorney turned her attention to Rand. Clearly, Michelle wanted to know where he stood.

"I don't want to spend all my time with Ginger fighting," he admitted. "So if it will help to work out all this stuff now, then I'm all in."

GINGER EXPECTED THE meeting would last for at least another hour. Instead, Rand suddenly thanked Michelle and promised to make another appointment as soon as they had all the information ready for her to peruse.

Their attorney thought that was a good idea. It would save them on their legal fees, as she was billing them at her hourly rate.

Ginger did not want to pay more than she had to, for services. So she thanked Michelle and rose, too.

Moments later she and Rand were walking out into the spring sunshine. He had been in a mood all day. Quiet and brooding. He kept looking at her, too.

That was probably because he'd apparently had to carry her to bed the night before, when she'd fallen asleep in the bathroom. That was no surprise. In the past few weeks she had been falling asleep more readily and more often than usual. It was, she had learned, a symptom of pregnancy in the first trimester.

Her overabundance of emotions, too. Which was why, she guessed, she had gotten all weepy after they'd made love the night before.

Part of it, of course, was the fact it was their wedding night that wasn't really a wedding night. At least not in the genuine traditional sense. And the other part was that, if things were different, she could easily see herself falling in love with him.

And she knew she couldn't let that happen.

Not when the two of them had such different outlooks on life.

Aware he was studying her, in that same careful analytical way, Ginger asked the first question that came to mind. "Why did you cut that meeting short?"

"Because clearly we have some talking to do, and I didn't want to do it in front of anyone else. Besides—" he pushed an errant strand of hair from her cheek "—it's been a long couple of days, and you're looking a little worn around the edges."

Ginger made an unappreciative face. "Thanks."

"You're also pr—"

She touched her finger to his lips before he could finish saying the word.

He stopped, his lips pressed evocatively against her index finger.

Aware this was as close to a kiss as she wanted to get, now or at any other time in the future, Ginger swiftly dropped her tingling hand and stepped back.

Still holding her gaze with a wickedly sensual one of his own, Rand continued. "I figured you could use a little nap before we combine places."

Lovely. He was bossing her around. Again.

Ginger propped her hands on her hips. "Is this how it's going to be? You're going to 'little lady' me every chance you get?"

Rand cupped her elbow and guided her toward his truck. "If you mean look out for your best interests…"

"I mean treat me like some hapless female who doesn't have enough sense to do anything without your interference."

He opened the passenger-side door. "Women in your situation need sleep."

"How do you know?" She took in the day's growth of beard on his ruggedly chiseled face. It seemed impossible that he could be more handsome now, in khakis and a button-down shirt, than he had been in a tuxedo the night before, but he was.

Rand shrugged; the happy gleam in his eyes at odds with his solemn tone. "I've been reading up on it since you told me you were carrying my child."

Wow...that certainly was unexpected. But putting a romantic spin on this could only lead to more trouble.

"Well, there's no reason to get all worked up about it." Ginger put her right foot on the running board, grabbed the handle above the window and swung herself gracefully up into the passenger seat. "It's just a temporary medical condition, easily managed by me."

Rand circled around and slid behind the wheel. "Well, too bad, then." He turned to smile at her. "Because you're going to have me looking out for both of you whether you want me there or not."

Ginger glared at him. He regarded her steadily and calmly in return. Okay, maybe she was being a tad overemotional. Again. Whether she wanted to admit it or not, the thought of a nice cozy bed and comfy nap pillow was enticing. But that would come later, when she had finished the tasks she had to do in the meantime.

Ginger released a beleaguered breath. "So where are we going to live?"

"Whoa!" Rand chuckled as he fit his key in the ignition. "You're actually agreeing to share space with me?"

Ginger flushed self-consciously. "Everyone will expect it."

"So that's the only reason you want to reside under the same roof?"

"Truthfully? Yes, it is."

Another silence fell, this one taut with a different kind of tension.

Rand turned the air-conditioning on high. "The closest available rental home is fifty miles away."

Somehow she wasn't surprised he had checked into that. When it came to getting her under his roof—and back into his bed—he was always thinking ahead. "Not good when we're talking mountain terrain." The commute to Summit and back could be an hour or more each way, every day.

Rand draped his arm across the back of the seat. "I do still have my cottage at the Red Sage guest ranch. I've been renting it by the week for the past four months."

Ginger had to admit it would be roomier—and less intimate—than the hotel room where she'd been staying. "Okay."

In less than an hour they'd packed her stuff and checked her out of the Summit Inn. She followed him in her truck out to the Red Sage.

Twenty-five minutes outside of Summit, the guest ranch encompassed twenty-nine-thousand acres of juniper and ponderosa-pine forest, wildflower-strewed meadows, red-rock canyon and stately mountains. The sprawling century-old ranch house was located at the end of a blacktop road half a mile from the rural highway. The three-dozen cottages surrounded a large party barn, where weddings and receptions were often held. Campsites were located near the end of the private hiking and biking trails.

Rand parked in front of Cottage 12. The one-story build-

ing had clapboard siding, red shutters and door, and a slop-
ing slate-gray roof. Ginger situated her truck beside his.

Both got out. "There's a complimentary breakfast buffet every morning in the main house. Otherwise we're on
our own for meals. There's also a coin laundry and an ice
and vending machine area."

He opened the door to the cottage and led the way inside.
The front appeared to be one large room sporting a small
galley kitchen and combination dining room–living area
with a fireplace. Behind it was a bathroom and one bedroom just large enough to house a queen-size bed, tall bureau and a nightstand. Behind that was a small porch with
a slow-moving fan overhead. Screened for privacy with
latticework and attractive landscaping that featured native
shrubs and flowering plants, there was an old-fashioned
porch swing meant for two, a comfy-looking chaise longue
and two small side tables.

All together, the cottage encompassed about seven hundred square feet, the size of a normal one-bedroom apart-
ment.

Ginger looked at the bed. There was no way she and her
six-foot-plus husband could sleep in it without touching.
And touching led to...

She *really* had to stop fixating on that.

"What do you think about us getting two cottages, side
by side?" she asked casually as she walked back into the
safety of the main living area.

Rand followed her. Evidently not at all surprised by her
question, he shrugged his broad shoulders. "It'd be a good
way to convince people we're not really married, if that's
what you're aiming to do."

Ginger sighed.

There were two wing chairs and a love seat in the living
room; no sofa large enough to sleep on. She raked a hand

through her hair, trying not to think how cozy and romantic this all would be under other circumstances. Now it just felt much too small and close. "I suppose a roll-away bed is out of the question, then?"

He nodded; a solid wall of masculine determination. "Completely."

The sensuality in his gaze had her heartbeat picking up, big time.

"It's not as if we haven't shared a mattress before," Rand pointed out, hovering closer to her.

Ginger suddenly felt as if the air had been sucked out of her lungs. "I know."

His gaze narrowed. "But…?"

Ginger swallowed, and pushed the wealth of erotic memories away. Just because they had recklessly made love the night before did not mean they would be doing so again. She wet her lips and said bluntly, "I was hoping to keep this on business terms."

He remained stoic. Not protesting. Not agreeing. Not… anything.

Wishing she knew more about what their immediate future held, she finally relented. "But…I guess this will do." *It would have to.*

Slowly the tension eased from his tall, ruggedly handsome frame. He offered a reassuring smile, his victorious attitude evident. "Let's get the rest of your stuff in. Then I'll go over to the front office and let Claire McPherson, the manager, know we're newlyweds and you'll be staying here with me. And I'll get you a key."

Settling in was easy, Ginger thought. Making this temporary union of theirs a success, while keeping her pregnancy hidden, would not be as simple.

Chapter Five

Rand had known sharing quarters with Ginger would be challenging. However, he hadn't expected her to be so contrary about every little thing.

"You don't have to leave all your things in the suitcases," he told her. "You can unpack."

Ginger struggled to fit her bags into her half of the closet. It wasn't an easy fit and took another hard shove to shut the door.

He lounged against the lone bureau, arms crossed in front of him.

Scowling, Ginger grabbed her handbag and perched on the edge of the bed. A curtain of copper hair fell across one shoulder as she pulled out a notepad and pen.

"What are you doing?" he asked.

Ginger scribbled. "Adding another requirement for our marriage contract." She paused to look up at him. "No unsolicited advice."

He let out a conciliatory breath. "Sorry. I wasn't trying to boss you around. I just wanted you to feel welcome here, like this was your place now, too." Given the fact that a week-by-week rental was the closest either of them got to an actual home these days, she had to concede.

Abruptly her shoulders lost their rigid tilt. Her expression softened, too. "So we're in agreement about this?"

"Yes." He gave her a level look and did his best to re-assure her. "There will definitely not be any bossing each other around."

Her lips curved into a smile. "Good. Because I don't want to waste time arguing with you."

"I don't want to argue with you, either," he said quietly. Their gazes remained locked. Intimacy followed. As was always the case, though, before they could take their relationship one step further, something inevitably got in the way. His cell phone rang and it was followed shortly thereafter by the ring on hers.

Ginger stepped outside to answer the call.

Rand stayed in the cottage and listened to his caller. "That's great news!" he exclaimed. "Yes. I'll be there." He severed the connection.

Seconds later Ginger stepped inside. "The county's moratorium on horizontal drilling has just been lifted," she announced joyfully. She came closer in a drift of floral and citrus perfume. "Dot and Clancy Boerne are having a meeting at their ranch this evening."

Uh-oh, Rand thought. "I know."

Ginger paused. "You were invited?"

He nodded, aware they had hit the first professional hurdle in their marriage. "The Boernes have asked me to analyze the environmental impact of all the proposals from wildcat drilling operations."

Ginger's jaw took on the stubborn tilt he knew so well. "Well, you can't do that."

"Why not?"

"Because I'm bidding on that work!" she snapped.

More than that, Rand knew, she was counting on winning the contract to launch her career as an independent oil woman.

Ginger continued hotly, "You're going to have to re-cuse yourself."

Rand had to draw the line somewhere. He figured it may as well be here. Especially since she was the one who was actually carrying their child, and hence would eventually be out of commission, at least for a short time. "How about *you* recuse yourself?"

More temper flared. "I'm not letting this opportunity go, Rand."

He shrugged, knowing she would receive income from this project only if she won it, whereas his fees were guaranteed. "I gave the Boernes my word I would thoroughly review every proposal to let them know the risks. I will be operating with a panel of three others. I've been working with them and many others in the county for months now, to ensure land and interests are protected. I'm not backing out."

Ginger strode farther away. "Well, neither am I."

He studied her, clearly disappointed. He had hoped she would be more reasonable. Clearly this wasn't the case. "Then I suggest," he said mildly, "that you accept this is just the way it's going to be."

HAD THE COMPLICATIONS ended there, it would have been a tough but not ultimately insurmountable problem, Ginger thought.

Unfortunately when they got to the meeting at the Boerne ranch, and saw who else was in attendance, she realized her woes were just beginning.

Not only did she have her new husband looking over her shoulder in a professional sense, she apparently had her new mother-in-law interested in acquiring the work, too. Because Josie Corbett-Wyatt McCabe—the current head of Wyatt Drilling—sauntered onto Dot and Clancy Boerne's lawn just as the meeting was about to begin and took a seat on the opposite side of the large outdoor gathering.

Feeling like a player in a minor league team, who had just had a major league player show up and push her out of her long-coveted spot, Ginger turned to Rand in shock. "Did you know your mom was coming tonight?"

"No." He stared at his mother, clearly ticked off.

Josie stared back at her son, giving no quarter, either.

As far as Rand's mother was concerned, Ginger noted, this was business, pure and simple. Family connections did not enter into it.

Ginger couldn't help but admire that about Josie. She felt that way, too. It was only Rand who seemed to think they should make exceptions.

Before she had a chance to think about the best way to handle what was bound to be an uncomfortable situation, yet another man joined the hundred-plus oil people on the lawn.

As their eyes locked, it was all Ginger could do not to groan out loud. Not him, too.

Rand took in the latest arrival's air of cool detachment. Unlike most of the other oil folk there that evening, clad in jeans, boots and work shirts, the VP from the midsize oil company wore designer jeans, a trendy sport coat and a tie.

Tensing, Rand leaned down to murmur in her ear, "Do you two know each other?"

"Kind of."

Rand waited.

"He's my ex-husband. Conrad Profitt."

Rand blinked in a way that let her know he could hardly believe his ears. Which wasn't surprising, she supposed. Since they had only referred to their exes by their first names, he had no way of putting two and two together until now.

"Your first husband was the heir apparent of Profitt Oil?" he asked in stunned amazement.

"Yep."

Another pause. "Did you know he was going to be here tonight?"

"Nope." Ginger took in Conrad's pompous, self-congratulatory air. Could this situation get any more complicated?

Meanwhile their hosts called the meeting to order. The brawny, white-haired rancher stepped to the makeshift-podium, while his petite and pretty wife passed out folders to all the guests. Clearly ready to get on with it, Clancy Boerne began. "We asked you all here tonight because we want to give you a chance to recover the oil on our property. The deadline for submitting drilling plans, cost estimates and proposed oil-lease terms is three weeks from this evening."

Next, Clancy introduced the three experts on seismic mapping, directional drilling and recovery performance that he and his wife had hired to help them sift through the proposals.

Finally he introduced the fourth and last member of their advisory panel—the lone environmentalist in the group. Clancy smiled. "You all know Rand McCabe. He's been working closely with the county commissioners and many of the ranchers in the area to help us protect our properties. Rand will vet the proposals, from an environmental standpoint, and report back to us on any insufficiencies and dangers.

"My wife, our attorney and I will go over the results of both that and the independent financial and engineering analysis. The top ten bidders will then be asked to further explain and/or defend their proposals in a question-and-answer session at our attorney's office. The panel of three experts will assist us in the questioning, and another comprehensive analysis will be completed. After that point, we'll decide which outfit to use and notify everyone by telephone a few days later."

Conrad Profitt raised his hand and asked sagely, "Does anyone else see a problem with Rand McCabe vetting his own mother's bid?"

Ginger turned to look at her ex-husband, not surprised Conrad was already crying foul. Whenever her ex felt he couldn't win on his own, which was most of the time, he used whatever device he could to level the playing field. In this case the hint of familial impropriety.

At the podium, Boerne scoffed at the concern. "The only one who should have a problem with Rand being involved is Josie Corbett-Wyatt McCabe—since she's had her son interfere in more of her drilling projects than she can probably count."

Everyone chuckled, knowing that truer words had never been spoken. The rift in the McCabe clan over *that* long-standing issue was legend. Turns out, Rand was as cautious as his mother was fearless.

Another independent oilman promptly raised his hand. "What about Rand's new wife, Ginger Rollins?" he demanded. "You telling me McCabe's going to be as hard on her as everyone else, them being newlyweds and all?"

Rand's expression remained impassive, while Ginger grimaced. She hadn't wanted her new marriage to come up tonight at all, at least not in a business sense.

Meanwhile, Ginger's ex stared at her in astonishment. Clearly, Profitt hadn't heard.

Nor had most of the people there.

Figuring any defense should come from her, Ginger stood and addressed the crowd. "I guarantee you that Rand will be as tough on me as he is on everyone else."

Despite her avowal, skepticism abounded.

Dot Boerne took the floor. "We're going to have the names on all the bids redacted by our oil-and-gas attorney before we see the proposals. Rand and the other advisors will not have access to that information, either. The winning semifinal bids will be chosen strictly on the merits of ingenuity, environmental safety and cost."

"What about the final round?" someone asked.

Dot said, "Obviously, we'll know who we are dealing with then, since we'll expect all the executives and field experts from the various companies to be at the Q and A sessions."

Clancy Boerne added that in the end he and Dot would choose the company they were most comfortable with.

More questions followed. Eventually the meeting concluded.

Conrad ambled over to Ginger and Rand. She couldn't be sure, but she thought her ex's head of meticulously groomed brown hair might be thinning a tad.

Her ex-husband stuck out his hand to Rand. "It appears congratulations are in order."

"They are." Rand amenably shook the oil tycoon's hand, then stepped back and put a proprietary arm around Ginger's shoulders, tugging her close to his side.

Still flummoxed, Conrad turned his full attention back to his ex-wife. "I had no idea you were serious about anyone."

"Nor should you have since we haven't spoken in—what? Two years?"

Conrad's smile broadened. "We should remedy that," he said.

Ginger had an idea what her ex-husband wanted, and it wasn't friendship. "I disagree." She turned to Rand, deriving comfort from his muscular warmth despite herself.

She slipped her arm around his waist and looked up at her new husband adoringly. "You ready to go, sweetheart?"

Taking her hint, Rand smiled. "I sure am, honeybunch." Still holding Ginger protectively close, he pivoted and gave Ginger's ex a two-fingered salute. "Nice to meet you, Profitt."

They walked off, arm in arm, only to be stopped again several steps later. Everyone, it seemed, wanted to talk about their newly married state. More questions and congratulations followed. Finally they made their way to the rows of cars and trucks parked along the lane that led to the ranch house.

To Ginger's chagrin, Josie McCabe was waiting next to her pickup, her manner all business. Ginger sighed. The last thing she wanted to discuss with her new mother-in-law was the cutthroat competition ahead.

Rand paused beside Josie's canary-yellow truck. He looked as tense and irritable as Ginger felt, although for more complicated familial reasons. "Since when have you been interested in drilling in Summit County?" he asked his mother.

Josie sent her youngest son a look of reproach. "Since they came out with the massive improvements in horizontal drilling technology last fall. I knew there had been problems in the past when that method of oil recovery was tried here. I also knew, with the amount of oil beneath the ground, that it would be only a matter of time before it commenced again, safely this time." She turned slightly, leveling them both with her sturdy gaze. "I've always intended to be in on the ground floor of the boom in Summit County."

And yet her son remained unconvinced. "I've never seen you here, going ranch to ranch, like everyone else," Rand said.

Josie shrugged. "I came down last summer, ahead of everyone else, and made my connections then."

Of course, Ginger thought. A lady wildcatter as successful as Josie McCabe would not let an opportunity like this one go unexplored. "Which is why you were invited to hear the Boernes' stipulations on the bid process for their ranch." Because Josie had already laid the groundwork.

Josie nodded. "Luckily, I'd heard the rumors the moratorium was about to be lifted. So I was already here."

"And yet you didn't say anything, when you saw us yesterday, about coming back to Summit," Rand persisted, clearly unhappy. "Even when you knew that Ginger and I were returning today."

Josie's gaze narrowed with maternal rebuke. "I didn't want you to think I planned to interfere in your marriage. Because I don't. And I didn't think it was a good idea for us to be arguing business on your wedding day."

"It's not a good idea for family to be arguing, period," Ginger put in.

Never mind hovering around each other, under difficult circumstances, such as these.

"I agree." Josie straightened, her manner brisk. "That is why I think *you* should recuse yourself, Rand. Let some other environmental impact engineer advise the residents of Summit County."

Ginger looked at Josie, surprised and relieved to find them so like-minded. "That's exactly what I told him," she blurted.

Although that still left her and her new mother-in-law angling for the very same work, which wasn't a good situation, either.

Rand harrumphed. "I'm not bowing out unless both of you also remove yourselves from the bidding process. And

I don't see that happening." He paused, giving Ginger and Josie a hard, assessing look. "Do you?"

RAND EXPECTED GINGER to give him the silent treatment once they settled in his pickup. Instead she turned to him and asked, "Do you know what is in the fridge back at the cottage? I didn't have a chance to look."

He sighed. "Condiments and beverages, mostly."

She glanced at her watch. "The grocery store in Summit is open until ten. Do you mind if we stop there before we head back to Red Sage?"

Rand's mood brightened. This was the first thing she'd done that was the slightest bit domestic, and he liked seeing this side of her. "Sure. No problem."

While he drove, she plucked the notepad and pen from her bag and made a list. She tore it in two as they headed inside. "If we each take a basket, it will be faster."

And, Rand noted, they needed to be quick since they only had fifteen minutes until closing. It took every moment of that to get the items she had assigned him. When they met up at the line, the clerk rang up the items, he paid, and Ginger bagged.

Only when they got back to the cottage did he have a chance to really see what they had purchased. Steak, chicken, ground beef. Lots of fresh produce and fruit. Cereal. Milk. Juice. Several kinds of flour and sugar, spices and other baking items. Eggs.

"You planning to cook?"

"Are you?"

He lifted an affable shoulder. "I can grill."

"Well, I can do everything else."

"Sounds like a plan," he said cheerfully.

Ginger finished putting the refrigerator items away, then picked up the lone bag of chocolate sandwich cookies and a gallon of milk, and carried them, along with a glass, to the dining table.

She disappeared for a moment. He heard her hauling her suitcase out of the closet. More activity followed, then she came out with a bottle of prenatal vitamins in her hand. "Doctor's orders," she explained as she sank onto a chair and kicked off her shoes.

Rand moved to join her at the table. "Actually, there's something I've been meaning to ask you…" He cleared his throat, feeling oddly out of sorts. "Have you had any morning sickness yet?"

"Thankfully…no. I'm hoping to dodge that bullet altogether. I have friends who have been green around the gills for their entire pregnancy, and that would put a definite crimp in my work schedule." Relaxing with a mixture of fatigue and relief, Ginger poured herself a tall glass of milk, downed a vitamin and then opened the bag of cookies.

Brow furrowing, she studied the interior of the package.

"Is there a problem?"

"I'm deciding how many to eat."

He loved the fact she was, and probably always would be on some level, a total mystery to him. He also loved how cute she looked when she was mildly perplexed. He sauntered closer. "Are we rationing them?"

She wrinkled her nose and returned, in the same deadpan tone, "If I had as many as I wanted, I'd eat the whole package in one sitting."

Rand laughed, not surprised she was greedy when it came to pure pleasure. So was he. He pulled out a chair, turned it around, sank onto it and folded his arms along the back. "So how many are you going to partake in, then?"

While she considered, Ginger let out a sexy little sigh. "Mmm. Two is too little, six is too much, even though there are six in the individual snack packs they sell." Her luscious lower lip pushed out in a delectable pout. She squinted, still thinking, and finally said, "Probably four." Decision made, she took four from the center row of the package.

Rand took four, too, from the same row, leaving complete rows on either side of the pillaged one. "I haven't had these in a while." He got up to get a glass for himself.

"Me, either. But I got to thinking about them while we were waiting for the meeting to start." She opened up a cookie and licked the vanilla cream out of the middle.

Rand nearly groaned.

The milk he was pouring splashed over the rim. Ignoring the hardness pressing against his fly, he grabbed a dishcloth and mopped up the mess. Returning to the table, he sat opposite her. "Is it your first craving?"

Ginger made a face, clearly resenting his question. "Hey." She lifted a staying hand. "I'm trying not to be a cliché."

Rand watched, his mouth dry, as she dunked a chocolate circle into the milk, swished it around delicately, and then popped the soggy confection into her mouth.

"You could never be a cliché." Unbearably sexy and sensual, yes.

Oblivious to the ardent nature of his thoughts, and the growing hardness of his lower body, she shot him a skeptical look and sighed. "You say that now…"

He meant it now. She was without a doubt the most fascinating and infuriating woman he had ever met. The woman he wanted most to bed…with or without his wedding ring on her finger.

Ginger sighed and broke open another chocolate sandwich cookie. "But when my mother finds out…"

He studied the troubled sheen to her dark green eyes, the slight tremble of her lower lip. "You think your mom will be happy about the baby?" he asked softly.

Ginger groaned. "Over the moon." She patted Rand on the hand, then stood. Finished with her snack, she headed for the bedroom. "And that, 'honeybunch,'" she drawled over her shoulder, mocking his earlier faux endearment, "is when the trouble starts."

Rand had no idea what Ginger meant by any of that. But sensing she needed her space, he let her have her privacy, only heading for bed when he was certain she was sound asleep.

WHEN HE WOKE the next morning, a little after dawn, she was already up. Papers, computer, maps spread all over the living area of their cottage.

She was still in her pajamas, glossy hair knotted on top of her head, a mug of decaf coffee in her hand. A pan of cold oatmeal was on the stove. "You know there's a free breakfast buffet at the main house every morning," he reminded her.

She nodded.

"We could go over together."

She barely looked up from the mounds of data she was studying. "No time." She flashed a wan, distracted smile. "You go ahead. And don't come into my temporary office. I don't want you looking at any of my plans until the Boernes ask you to do so."

He lifted a palm. "Firewall. I swear."

"Good."

Rand went to breakfast, ate and brought her something back.

She looked at the plate he carried in stunned amazement.

"In case you get hungry later."

For a second she looked longingly at the quiche and fruit salad, then went right back to what she had been doing. "Thanks, that looks really good. Mind putting it the fridge?"

"No problem."

Aware he had his own appointments to keep that day, he headed out, only to come in contact with an attractive fifty-something brunette in their front yard. She was dressed in oversize denim work clothes and engineer-style boots. A backpack laptop case slung over one sturdy shoulder, her hands were filled with rolled-up maps.

Rand paused to tip his hat. "Maria Gonzales, I presume?" He recalled Ginger mentioning the previous night that her drilling partner, a happily married woman with three teenage sons, would be here every day, working with her. And this woman sure fit the bill.

Dark eyes twinkled. "And you must be the never-stops-working-either Rand McCabe—the guy who finally got Ginger to settle down again."

Rand didn't know about that. His new wife still seemed to have both feet as far out the door as she could get, without raising any more eyebrows than they already had.

Maria put her maps down long enough to shake Rand's hand. "I never thought I'd see the day, but I'm glad I am. Ginger needs a big strong hunk of burnin' love like you to spice up her life." She winked. "And the fact you're doing it with wedding rings on your fingers is even better."

Ginger appeared in the doorway. Her elegant cheekbones were highlighted with a rosy-pink flush. "Rand and I may be hitched—"

Temporarily, he could see that his new wife wanted to add, but wisely didn't, lest she blow their cover.

"—but that doesn't mean anything important about our lives is going to change," Ginger finished, stubborn as ever.

The long-married Maria chuckled, picked up her maps

and turned back to Rand. "I see you've both still got some 'adjusting' to do," she teased.

Rand nodded, and just for the fun of it, hauled Ginger to him for a long, sexy, off-to-work kiss. "Uh-huh, and I'm aiming to help my beloved do just that." He lowered his head and, ignoring Ginger's soft gasp of surprise, pressed a hand to her spine and staked his claim with another steamy liplock.

Clearly shaken, Ginger broke off the kiss. Temper only he could see glittering in her dark green eyes, she flattened her hand across his chest and gave him a playful nudge, meant to throw off their audience. "Fun as this has been," she feigned sweetly, "it's time you went to task on something else."

"What could be more important for a still-honeymooning couple than this?" Rand bantered back. He grinned, and just for the hell of it, he kissed his wife again, even *more* passionately this time. Her flush turned even deeper but there was no denying the subtle shift and surrender of her supple body, nestled against his. Eventually though, knowing they both had much to do, he let her go. "See you later," he said. And heard only Ginger's huff of embarrassment, and Maria's laughter, as he strolled on down the walk.

WHEN RAND RETURNED that evening, he expected to find Ginger and Maria still hard at work. Instead Maria's van was gone and there was a familiar white Cadillac in front of their cottage with the license plate #1TXMOM, and a small U-Haul behind it.

Beside it was a yellow pickup with the vanity plate WILDCAT.

Rand stared at the vehicles in shock. Had Ginger known about any of this? If so, she hadn't said anything about expecting either of their mothers to come by.

He cut the ignition, got out and headed for the front door. He did not know what was going on, but he sure as heck was going to find out.

Chapter Six

"Mom, please…" Ginger's tired voice floated out the open cottage window.

Rand tensed at Cordelia's reply.

"Honey, I'm sorry, but I have to be honest with you. I do not want to see you make the same mistakes that you made in your first marriage." There was a long pause. "And from the looks of things, you've started your second marriage off on the wrong foot, too."

"I really think," he heard his mother interrupt kindly, "that all is not what it may seem."

Figuring enough had been said, Rand walked through the front door.

Ginger was standing in front of the workstation she had made for herself, her hair still damp from the shower and coiled in a loose messy knot on top of her head. She was clad in one of his blue chambray shirts and a pair of her comfortable-looking khaki cargo pants and socks. She wore no makeup but looked sexy as all get-out, just the same.

Rand nodded at the three women. "Nice to see everyone." He strode straight toward Ginger, took her in his arms and gave her the kind of kiss you would expect two people who were still technically in the honeymoon phase of their relationship, to give each other; the kind of kiss he had tried to give her that very morning.

This once, Ginger did not resist the open display of their passion. Maybe because she was as eager for respite from the familial scrutiny as he was.

Finished, Rand lifted his head. He caught the plea for help in her green eyes, then turned back to their mothers.

"So, what did I interrupt?" he asked.

Josie spoke first. "Cordelia called me while she was driving down, for directions to the place where you were staying. Since I just took a cottage here, I agreed to meet up with her in Summit and lead her out to the Red Sage." She grimaced. "Unfortunately, there are no more cottages to be had. Hotel rooms, either, at the moment. Which is why I walked down to offer Cordelia lodging in my cottage this evening."

Rand had to hand it to his mother. She might be a thorn in his side at times, but she also knew when to come to the rescue.

Ginger looked at Rand. "I also told Mom she could spend the night with us."

"But I don't think it's a good idea to impose on newly-weds," Cordelia told him demurely, "so I accepted Josie's invitation."

Thanks, Mom, Rand thought, telegraphing her a grateful look. "How long are you staying?" he asked his new mother-in-law.

"Just this evening. I have to be back at work the day after tomorrow, but I wanted you and Ginger to have all the wedding gifts that have poured in for you."

Ginger smiled pointedly at Rand. "I tried to tell Mom we don't need any of those things at the moment…"

"And I told my daughter," Cordelia explained, "that all the gifts will help her to properly set up housekeeping, wherever the two of you end up."

Rand looked out the window. The U-Haul trailer attached to Cordelia's Cadillac looked small, but he knew from experience just how much the 5 x 8 compartment could hold.

"But not to worry. I've already sent thank-you notes for the two of you, too."

Rand blinked in surprise.

"Mom thinks of *everything*," Ginger allowed tightly.

Cordelia caught the irritation underlying her daughter's too bright tone, and swung back to her only child. She propped her bejeweled hands on her hips. "You're telling me that you and Rand would have had time to do that in the next month?"

Actually, Rand thought, they wouldn't have.

"Those notes had to go out," Cordelia huffed.

"And we thank you for it," Rand said. If this was an example of Cordelia's usual helicopter parenting, no wonder Ginger was so flummoxed.

With an even brighter smile, Josie tried to push things along. "Back to the U-Haul."

Rand jumped in before the situation deteriorated further, suggesting, "How about I do the heavy lifting and bring everything in?"

Cordelia beamed. "You're such a dear."

"I'll go with you." His mother followed him outside and down the short stone path to the vehicles. Together, they walked around the Cadillac and opened up the trailer. It was packed to the gills. As was, apparently, the trunk and interior of Cordelia's Cadillac. Some of the gifts were still in shipping boxes, others just the store packaging. Rand handed one of the smaller boxes, marked Fragile, to his mother. "So what was going on back there before I walked in?" he asked casually.

Josie gestured for him to hand her one more. "Mother-daughter squabble."

The distressed look on Ginger's face said it had been much more. Rand took a large, heavy box marked Cookware. "Who was winning?" he mused.

Boxes balanced under her chin, Josie pivoted and headed up the walk. "Who do you think?"

As they neared the open window, Rand could hear female voices rising inside the cottage once again. He said, "I wouldn't count Ginger out."

"I'm not." A new respect laced Josie's low tone.

Their eyes meeting, they paused on the sidewalk. "Do me a favor?" Rand asked.

His mom nodded, amenable.

"Do whatever you have to do to divert Cordelia so I have time to talk to Ginger alone."

"YOU'RE SURE YOU want to go out for dinner this evening?" Cordelia asked a good twenty minutes later when all the boxed wedding gifts had been brought inside and stacked together in neat rows on the screened-in porch. It was the only place in the small abode where they could even hope to be out of the way.

With a smile, Rand jumped in to persuade her. "It will be a chance for the four of us to get to know each other better."

"But we'll need to get cleaned up first," Josie commented, linking her arm through Cordelia's. "So let's walk down to my cottage." She smiled. "We'll stop by the office on the way, and speak to them about bringing in a roll-away bed."

"I noticed a Help Wanted sign in the window, when I drove in." Cordelia sounded worried. "Is the service here substandard, because of that?"

Rand caught his mother's most patient smile as the two women exited and shut the screen door behind them. "I believe that posting has to do with the party barn operation," Josie replied as their voices faded. "But we can certainly talk to Claire McPherson…"

Finally silence fell. The spring breeze blew through the open windows. Ginger looked at Rand, then the over-whelming amount of cardboard boxes, and let out a groan. "I don't have time to mess with any of this."

Nor should she have to, Rand thought.

He sat next to her on the love seat and took her hand in his. "It's not that big a deal. We'll take whatever you need out of them and put the rest in storage."

"When? I still have work to do tonight."

As did he.

He patted her arm. "Look, the gifts are fine where they are now, on the porch. We'll get to them when we get to it."

"I suppose that'll work…for now." Still looking dis-traught, Ginger ran her fingers through her damp hair. "I wasn't planning to go out to dinner."

Nor was he. He'd been hoping to have a night alone with his new bride, maybe figure out a way to get her back into his arms, wanting to make love with him again.

He pushed aside his own selfish desires. "It's just one evening. You heard your mother—she's leaving in the morning." The two of them could deal with it. Especially if a good "performance" this evening appeased Cordelia and hence kept her from trying to "help" even more.

Another long, discouraged look. Ginger plucked the hair dryer from her suitcase, plugged it in and began blowing the residual dampness from the gleaming copper strands.

Enjoying the sight of her getting ready to go out, some-thing he wasn't usually treated to, he perched on the edge of the bed and watched.

Ginger bent from the waist. As she ran the dryer over

the underside of her hair, her shirt gaped in front, giving him a very nice view of cleavage and lace.

Rand felt himself hardening again. A perpetual state of affairs...

"She's trying to control my life," Ginger complained, pouting as she switched off the hair dryer.

Rand shrugged and stood to ease the pressure. "So don't let her." He walked around, willing the blood pooling low to dissipate.

"Easier said than done." Ginger shook her head. "You have no idea how smothering Mom can be, when she thinks—erroneously, I might add—that I desperately need her assistance." Wearily she went to the closet. Her large suitcase was open, the clothes inside a rumpled mess. Her hair tumbled over her shoulders as she studied the choices, then finally plucked out a white knit shirt and a relaxed-fit navy cardigan.

Rand ambled closer, offering a sexy wink. "Not going to wear my shirt?" He ran a finger down her cheek.

Ginger flushed and stepped back, her hand flying to the buttons. "Sorry about that."

Hungrily, he watched her undo one button, then another and another, as she swiftly undressed.

Suddenly she wasn't the only one wishing they didn't have plans for dinner out.

Unable to help himself, he moved close enough to see the shadowy valley between her soft, luscious breasts. Aware her spirits still needed bolstering, he bent and kissed the silky skin of her temple before giving her shoulder a reassuring squeeze. "Don't apologize. I like the way you look in it."

As elusive as ever, she danced away, slipped the shirt off and tossed it at him. He caught it and lifted it to his face. It was warm and soft and smelled the way she did—

fresh out of the shower—like orange blossom and shampoo and woman. Figuring there was no need to let any of that go to waste, when he needed a clean shirt, anyway, Rand removed the shirt he was wearing and slipped on the one she had been wearing.

Grinning despite herself, she shook her head at him. "Our mothers are going to know what you just did."

"So?" He waggled his eyebrows. "I don't mind sharing everything with you." *Including and especially a bed.*

Her mood improving, Ginger chuckled as she pulled the knit shirt over her head and then worked her arms through the sleeves. Her breasts, which seemed to get fuller every day now, were spilling out of the lacy bra. She tugged the white fabric down over her ribs, started to tuck it into the snug waistband of her otherwise loose-fitting cargo pants, then brought the shirt tail back out again to hide the slow but subtle changes in her slender body. She put the navy cardigan on and began buttoning.

"I really am sorry. I didn't mean to confiscate your wardrobe. But I was in the middle of a wardrobe crisis when I heard the knock at the door, and I still needed a shirt, so I grabbed the first oversize thing I saw."

"Which happened to be my shirt."

Ginger picked up her makeup bag and carried it to the bathroom mirror. "It's big enough to hide the very beginning of a baby bump."

He lounged against the portal, making a careful survey of her still-slender body, and watching her apply a thin layer of moisturizer to her freshly scrubbed face. "No one can tell you're pregnant." Even he was having trouble discerning the changes. And he'd made an art out of studying every delicious inch of her, even before they'd hit the sheets that very first time.

She flattened her free hand against her tummy and

checked out her profile in the mirror with a worried frown. "Yet."

Rand picked up his electric razor. Figuring he might as well get rid of the day's stubble, he ran it over his jaw. Finished, he reached for his toothbrush. "When do you want to tell our families?"

Ginger rooted through her cosmetics bag. "Not until it's so apparent we have no choice."

Fascinated, he watched her finish putting on her makeup. The process was quick; the results subtle but pretty. "I take it having your mom show up like this was not a happy surprise?"

Ginger put on a layer of gloss, then smacked her lips together. Finished, she reached for a pair of earrings and threaded them through her pierced lobes. The golden oil wells dangled sexily. "You see how my mom is reacting, and all we are is married?"

Rand nodded, aware the ultimate helicopter parent in Cordelia seemed to be operating on full speed.

Ginger shook her head miserably. "There's no telling how much she'll want to interfere when she finds out her first—and probably only—grandchild is on the way."

To GINGER'S RELIEF, the first half of dinner with their mothers went well. Josie and Rand kept the conversation squarely on things they could all agree upon, but eventually Ginger's mom brought the focus back to where she wanted it. The state of Ginger's new marriage.

"Honey, I don't mean to interfere—"

Famous last words, Ginger thought, bracing herself.

"—but I really think you ought to forget trying to get your own business going, and go to work for someone else. Or better yet, not work at all while the two of you get settled into a new routine."

"We're already settled," Ginger said.

Rand nodded. "I'm happy."

He certainly *looked* happy, Ginger thought, then quickly warned herself not to get too excited, given the fact that he was just living up to familial expectations, same as she.

With another smile of encouragement, Cordelia pushed on. "The point is, marriage is an adjustment and the newlywed phase is something to be savored, not rushed through blindly. Don't you agree, Josie?"

Put on the spot, Rand's mother paused. "I think Rand and Ginger know better than we do what they need, Cordelia."

"Still—" Cordelia ran a spoon through the frosting on her coconut cake "—it never hurts to take the time to get every detail set up properly."

Unable to stop herself, Ginger cut in. "We've already done that, Mom."

As always, Rand seemed to know where she was going almost before she did.

He gave her a look that advised her not to continue, but Ginger knew there was only one way to quiet her mother. "That's why Rand and I saw a lawyer about drawing up both a postnup, to cover the financials, and a marriage contract, to cover everything else that could possibly cause us problems down the line. Because neither of us has any intention of leaving anything to chance."

"Well, I have to hand it to you," Rand told Ginger an hour later, after they had returned to the Red Sage guest ranch, said good-night to the moms and retired to their "honeymoon" cottage. "You took mild parental concern to DEFCON levels of wariness, in a flash."

Glad the dinner was over, Ginger paused to toe off her boots. "It wasn't that bad."

Rand hunted around in the fridge and pulled out a bottle

of beer, left over from his "bachelor" days. He twisted off
the cap and sauntered closer. "Ah, yeah, it was. Especially
when you referenced your list and told them what was on
the agenda for the marriage contract so far."

Ginger looked longingly at the icy brew, then frowned
and headed for the cabinet. Ignoring his contemplative
gaze, she revealed, "My mother already thinks I'm completely misguided." She twisted the cap off the bottle she
had hidden behind the coffee cups and shook a prenatal
vitamin into her hand.

Rand lounged against the kitchen counter and watched
her pour a glass of milk. "And now she knows for sure?"

Ginger rolled her eyes at his teasing. She didn't know
how he did it, but her new husband could always coax a
smile from her, even under the most trying of circumstances.

"Your mother didn't say much about it." She paused
to swallow her vitamin, then made a face and went for a
chocolate sandwich cookie, as per usual, to kill the lingering iron taste of the supplement.

Rand admitted this was so with a tilt of his handsome
head, then took another swig of beer. He wiped his mouth
with the back of his hand. "That's because she was in
shock."

Ginger studied Rand over the rim of her glass, curious now. "Your family doesn't believe in prenups?" She
would think, with their wealth and influence, it would be
a no-brainer.

Rand watched her eat another cookie, just for the heck
of it. It had been a stressful evening, after all.

"McCabes believe in marrying for love." He moved
closer, lifted his finger and wiped a drop of milk from the
corner of her lip before ever so slowly lowering his hand
and stepping back. "And a love that is strong enough to

compel one of us to hitch our wagon to someone else's for the rest of our lives also requires a huge amount of trust. On everyone's part."

Tingling from his light, tender touch, Ginger shrugged and drained her glass. "Maybe that's the case under usual circumstances," she acknowledged. "But when all's said and done in *our* situation, they'll be thankful we've gone to the trouble to put everything in writing ahead of time."

After taking another slow, thoughtful sip of beer, Rand looked her over. "You're talking about our inevitable split?"

Ginger nodded. It was what they had agreed upon, what they both knew would happen. Yet to her surprise, she couldn't help feeling a little discomfited about it, too.

RAND WASN'T SURPRISED to see Ginger go right back to work that evening. He was a little annoyed by the continual chirping of her cell phone. Finally, around midnight, she shut it off. "Who keeps calling?"

Ginger grinned and reached for The List. She added No Monitoring Each Other's Calls to the marriage contract must-haves. Then sat back, her expression baiting. "You really want to know?"

Did he? And if so, what did that say about him?

He took a chair, set it a distance from her work area and lowered himself into it. "Yeah," he said, deciding to go with his gut, and satisfy his curiosity no matter how it looked. "I do."

"Three were texts from my mother."

"Everything okay?"

"She wants to have a private talk before she leaves in the morning about the ins and outs of being a good wife."

Ginger got up and stretched.

Somewhere in the course of the evening, she had changed into a pair of loose-fitting, pink-and-white-striped cotton pajamas. Her hair had been put up in a loose and messy knot on top of her head. Sexy copper tendrils curled against her nape and brushed at her temple and cheeks.

Rand stayed where he was with effort. "She's serious?"

Another sigh. Another slow, feline stretch. "Oh, yes." Her rueful smile upped his pulse. "My mom completely doted on my father. Her whole life revolved around making him happy, and when I was younger, taking care of me. She could anticipate our needs before we even knew what they were."

Ginger and Cordelia did not seem to be on the same page these days, Rand noted. "What happened to change that?"

Ginger stood feet apart, hands clasped behind her. She bent down, so her face was at her knees, and stretched the kinks out gently. "My dad died when I was a senior in high school. Massive heart attack. He was out on a rig on the Gulf, doing geological studies for a customer. He was dead before they could get him airlifted to a hospital on shore."

Rand could see how much that had hurt—and how much she did not want him to go to her and hold her right now. "I'm sorry," he said softly.

"Yeah." Briefly, sadness crossed her face. "It was tough. I still miss him to this day. Anyway, my mom was beside herself with grief. To make matters worse, I was leaving for Texas A&M that same summer. She asked me not to go, to skip a year and stay home in San Angelo with her, but I knew if I did, she'd never even begin to move on with her life. So I made the decision to go off to college anyway."

Rand noted the complex mixture of emotions on Ginger's face. Grief. Resentment. Most of all, she bore the look she had when she felt smothered with attention or pushed into a corner. "I'm guessing Cordelia didn't take it well?"

"She started driving up to see me a couple of times a week. Always, a surprise."

Rand recalled how much he had wanted independence in his first heady college days. "You resented it?"

Ginger nodded sharply. "Everyone was making fun of me, and I felt…suffocated. I was missing my dad, too, but I also needed to be on my own. Anyway, we had a big blow-up during fall break. I went off with a friend, rather than go home, and she was devastated. But I just… I couldn't take it. Our family doctor referred Mom to a grief support group and a therapist, and she eventually realized she had to have more in her life and went back to work as a party planner."

Impressed, Rand said, "No wonder she did such a good job with our surprise wedding."

Ginger smiled in agreement, and then went quiet.

"You really think Cordelia's going to be a problem for us?" he asked.

Ginger raked her teeth across her lower lip. "I hope not."

"But?" Rand persisted when she didn't go on.

Ginger lounged next to him against the counter. "Any time my mom senses I'm in a dilemma—or even at risk of *getting* in trouble—she starts becoming over-involved in my life again." She winced. "She says she just can't help it."

Rand tucked an errant strand of hair behind her ear. "You think she senses something is up with us, other than what we've told everyone?"

Ginger shook her head. She pivoted to face him, and as she moved, the notch collar of her pajama top crinkled, giving him a nice view of the uppermost curve of one lovely breast. "I think she wants to believe you're the love of my life, and vice versa, and that our impetuousness grew out of the passion we have for each other."

Rand had the idea that his mother, a real romantic at heart, had erroneously come to the same conclusion.

Ginger moved away again, taking with her the seductive glimpse of her breast. "My mom doesn't want us to lose sight of that…um…'passion' in all the drudgery and domesticity of day-to-day living, so she's trying to help me—us—keep our focus on what's important during our honeymoon phase."

Rand knew the one thing he did not need was any help remembering to covet his wife. That was an ever-present constant that had him physically uncomfortable whenever they were alone. "But you still want Cordelia to give you your space."

"Heck, yes!"

Rand wanted that, too. Otherwise, he would never have the time and opportunity to convince Ginger to make love with him again.

And again.

Ginger's brow furrowed as if she sensed the libidinous nature of his thoughts. "What are you thinking?" she demanded.

Already concocting his path to greater marital happiness, Rand grinned. "That for all our sakes, it's time you and I do a little more convincing."

Chapter Seven

"They're coming," Ginger announced as she stepped away from the window.

Rand held out his arms. Ginger went into them, and began kissing him passionately, just as they had planned.

It was supposed to be a staged kiss. Purely a means to an end. But, as always, the moment his lips touched hers, she felt a lightning bolt of desire soar through her. All coherent thought fled. Her only focus was the soft persuasive warmth of his mouth on hers, the strength in the arms around her and the hardness of his body pressed against hers.

A delicate cough sounded behind them.

Her blush of embarrassment all too real, Ginger turned to see their mothers standing on the other side of the screen door.

Rand flashed an unrepentant grin at both their moms. "Sorry." He shrugged. "Newlyweds."

Josie gave them an assessing glance that spoke volumes about the doubts she was privately having. "So we see," she said dryly.

Rand held the door open and ushered both women inside.

Cordelia admired the stand mixer, toaster and espresso maker they had set out on the counter. A nice set of cookware was sitting on top of the stove, ready to be put away. More boxes were opened. Meanwhile, Ginger's real work was nowhere in sight.

"You have been busy!" Cordelia beamed her approval.

Ginger nodded. "I realized you're right, Mom. I do need to pay more attention to making Rand happy."

Rand laced his hand around Ginger's waist. "And I need to make sure my beautiful bride has everything she wants and needs." He squeezed her affectionately, and kissed the top of her head. "Otherwise," he mused, "what's the point of being married?"

To their delight, Cordelia bought their ruse, hook, line and sinker—maybe because she was seeing what she wanted to see.

Rand's mother, though, was not such an easy sell.

"You want to tell me what's really going on?" Josie asked when she caught up with Rand in Summit later that day.

Rand paused, just outside city hall. "I'm happier than I've ever been?" The moment he spoke the words, he knew they were true.

"That, I can see. But I still think you and Ginger aren't telling us everything."

Rand shrugged. Waited.

Josie continued. "You're sure there's nothing else you want to tell me?"

He did. And he didn't. Finding out he was having a child—and with Ginger, to boot—was the best news he ever could have gotten. Part of him wanted to tell the world; the rest knew just how fragile his relationship with his new wife was. He didn't want to do or to say anything to put their growing closeness in jeopardy. Rand gestured amiably. "Nothing I can think of."

"Mmm-hmm."

Figuring now was the time to be frank about other matters, however, Rand continued. "Look, Mom, I know how much you love all your sons."

"I really do."

"I also know you've managed to let go of my brothers."

"Just not you?"

He smiled indulgently. "You worry when we're not happy."

"You got that right."

"But it's really not necessary. I'm a grown man. I can solve my own problems."

The tears his mom hadn't shed at his wedding to Ginger suddenly misted Josie's eyes. She squeezed his hand, said thickly, "Just so you know if you ever need advice or comfort you can still come to me."

A lump suddenly in his throat, too, Rand hugged her warmly. "Thanks, Mom. But you've got nothing to worry about."

And for the rest of the two weeks that followed, all went as smoothly as he had promised. Ginger worked nonstop on her proposal, Maria Gonzales by her side much of the time.

He met with many of the landowners in the area, who were interested in exploring their options, but—like Dot and Clancy Boerne—wanted to hire him to ensure their property was protected from an environmental standpoint. And it was only three days before the bids were due to be turned in, that conflict arose.

GINGER WAS JUST putting the finishing touches on the computer model of the drilling plan she had engineered for the Boernes when a knock sounded at her cottage door. She looked up from her computer and frowned at the person standing on the other side of the screen door. This, she thought, was what she got for leaving the main door open to let in the warm spring breeze.

"Got a minute?" Conrad asked.

Ginger knew that coolly calculating look. She turned away from her ex-husband, wondering yet again how she ever could have thought herself in love with him. "No."

"Give me five minutes of your time and I'll stop pestering you."

Ginger rose to unlock the door. But only because she knew Conrad would persist until he said what he had come to say. She ushered him inside, but left the main door open. Then stood contentiously between him and the oil-recovery plan she and Maria were going to submit.

Conrad removed his hat, slapped it against his thigh, and ran a hand through his thinning hair. "You're still ticked off at me, aren't you?"

Once again, he was dressed in a sport coat, designer jeans and tie. And of course shiny rattlesnake-skin boots that ran into the thousands of dollars. "Actually, I'm not." Truth was, she didn't really care what Conrad did, as long as she didn't have to see or hear from him. Not that this had been much of an issue thus far, given how acrimoniously the two of them had parted.

Looking slightly uncomfortable standing there, hat in hand, her ex-husband regarded her somberly. "The company made a mistake not taking you seriously."

Of course they had.

"Frankly, we should have done whatever was necessary back then to retain you," he continued.

Now, it was all beginning to make sense....

To succeed in the oil business, a person had to be good at mapping geologic strata and identifying mineral deposits, acquiring the land, and/or designing, supervising and completing major drilling projects. The best CEOs were talented in all three areas.

Conrad was a good land man. He had a knack for being able to talk to people and sign them up. However he struggled mightily in the other two areas. A fact his multitalented father had worried about, since Conrad would never be able to take his place at the helm unless the board of directors backed Conrad. And the board wouldn't do that unless Conrad had proved himself on a big project, which he had yet to do.

Ginger regarded her ex sagely. "Would you still be saying this if one of your top competitors *hadn't* struck oil in Ochiltree County, using a very similar strategy to the one I proposed?"

Conrad flashed his most persuasive smile. "The point is, Ginger, you had the right approach all along. My dad and I, and the rest of the VPs, were just too thickheaded and set in our ways to realize it."

"Okay." Ginger shrugged. She had some idea what this mea culpa was costing her egocentric ex. "Apology accepted."

Conrad eased closer and continued his pitch. "Profitt Oil wants you back, as VP of domestic exploration."

"That's a pretty big promotion."

He nodded, serious. "And this time, my father and I will personally see to it that we follow your drilling plans, starting with the bid for the Boerne ranch."

She knew they would, if Conrad could somehow take credit for it. But it no longer mattered. It hadn't for a long time.

She turned him down with a look, then ushered him toward the door. "Thanks for stopping by."

He dug in his heels. "Come on, Ginger. For once in your life, be reasonable! You know you haven't got a chance in hell of winning the bidding frenzy over the Boerne deal. Or any other worthwhile oil lease in this neck of the woods, for that matter!" His beseeching smile turned ugly. "Your drilling partner, Maria Gonzales, may have a stellar reputation, but you're too new at this, your resources as a fledgling independent too slim. The midsize companies and well-established wildcatters are going to get all the work."

Maybe so, but not for lack of trying on her part, Ginger thought stubbornly.

Glad that Maria—who was beginning to feel a little nervous about their chances of winning the job, too—had missed Conrad's confidence-busting speech, she said, "And here I thought you just showed up to flatter me." She opened the door, and pushed Conrad through it, right into Rand's imposing form.

Her current husband looked about as pleased as her former husband.

Rand scowled at Conrad. "I believe the lady asked you to leave."

Conrad took another few steps away from Ginger, then turned. "You don't have to run through the entire trust fund your dad left you to prove yourself," he told her. "You have other options, Ginger. At least you would if you weren't too foolish to consider them."

"That's not why I'm doing this!" Ginger retorted. She pivoted away from both men and stormed back inside.

In her wake, low voices rumbled unpleasantly on the stoop. One set of heavy male footsteps headed away from the screen door, the other walked in. Rand took a moment to look her over, head to toe.

Resisting the urge to throw herself into his arms, and let him hold her for as long as he wanted this time, Ginger stayed where she was.

Although she had gotten over her ex's betrayal and her

divorce a long time ago, she still felt frustrated, as well as a little embarrassed, by all the time she had wasted when she was with Conrad.

"You okay?" he asked quietly.

Taking a deep breath, she nodded. Her days of trying to win a man's respect were over. He either gave it to her or he didn't.

Squinting, Rand stepped a little closer to her. "How long was Profitt here?"

Ginger turned and hazarded a glance at her computer. "Any time at all is too long."

Silence fell as Rand waited for a more complete answer.

Her body warming as much as if he had actually touched her, Ginger finally replied, "Five minutes, maybe less." She pivoted toward Rand and studied him in return, wondering if that was a hint of jealousy—or wariness—in his blue eyes.

Knowing she probably would have felt the same if she'd caught him in a tête-à-tête with his ex, she asked, "How much did you hear?"

"Enough to know Conrad and his colleagues dismissed your drilling strategies out of hand when the two of you were working together."

She winced. "While pretending to take me seriously." That humiliation hurt the most.

"What made you realize he wasn't sincere?" The expression on his handsome face gentling, Rand stepped behind her and massaged the tense muscles between shoulder and spine.

The expert ministrations of his fingers was heavenly. Ginger shut her eyes and leaned into his soothing touch. She hadn't realized until that second how tense she was.

She released a contented sigh, then forced herself to continue relating the heartbreaking details of her past.

"I was checking my work mail on our home computer one day, and stumbled on an email between my ex and his father. His dad wanted to know when Conrad was going to convince me to quit working and get serious about producing some heirs to the family dynasty. Conrad had apparently promised his father it would be soon, but it wasn't soon enough for Conrad Senior's agenda. He urged his son in no uncertain terms to just get on with it, and bribe me with whatever he had to, to make it happen.

"Conrad wrote back and said he and I didn't work that way. And that he had the utmost confidence that I *would* come around eventually, but not until I got the oil business out of my system. Hence, Conrad wanted to keep humoring me a little while longer. Until I got fed up with constantly falling flat on my face and decided to quit and make babies."

Rand made a dissenting sound as he worked his way down to her waist, relaxing every taut sinew in his path. Reveling in his tender touch, Ginger shifted to allow him greater access. A little more of this wouldn't hurt, she told herself. After all, it wasn't as if they were making love. Besides, if she was this tense, wouldn't that mean their baby was tense, also?

"I gather you confronted your husband?" Rand asked eventually, kneading her lower back.

So relaxed now her knees were getting a little wobbly, Ginger nodded. "Conrad admitted he had never wanted me to work after we were married. He felt one career was enough for any couple."

Rand took her hand and guided her over to the love seat. His tone a husky murmur, he ventured, "You disagreed."

Ginger sank into the thick comfortable cushions. She watched as Rand took a seat beside her. Idly, she took his hand in hers and gave it a brief appreciative squeeze. "I saw what not having something of her own, to give her life purpose, did to my mother, over time. How much happier she was when she started working again and had a life outside of mine. I didn't want to travel the path she did." Ginger paused and bit her lip. "And I still don't."

"So what *do* you want?" he asked gently.

She turned her gaze to his. "I want it all. Satisfying career, family." *Love.* "And if I can't have that," *as she fully expected she probably would not, in the end,* "then I want to know I will always be able to support myself and my baby. That I don't need anyone else to do so." *Or,* she added silently, *anyone else to make me feel happy and complete. I want to do that on my own.*

Rand continued to study her thoughtfully. He kept her hand in his when she would have let his go. "First of all, it's *our* baby," he corrected her finally, his expression kind. "And you don't ever have to worry about having money to raise our child safely and comfortably because I will more than see to that."

Guilt flared in Ginger. Belatedly she realized how selfish she had just sounded.

Rand paused, his gaze roving her flushed cheeks. "Second, you'd have more of a nest egg if you held on to your inheritance from your dad and went to work for someone else."

Ginger knew that, too. She extricated her hand from his and stood. "But I wouldn't be independent, Rand. And for me—" she paused, looking intently into his eyes "—independence is key."

"IT'S GOING TO rain tonight."

Ginger looked up from the geological maps she had spread out over the dining table to see her husband framed in the doorway. Looking relaxed and still full of energy, he had one broad shoulder braced against the frame.

She'd spent so much time weighing the data and trying to pull together a coherent package that would not only address all potential problems, but recommend the best way to get the recovery factor above forty percent, that she was feeling a little woozy. And worn out.

"Why are you telling me?" Ginger asked, confused.

It wasn't as if she was outside or had been for days. Rand was the only one who had been going out to meet with clients. Her work was right here.

He inclined his head toward the screened-in back porch. The sun had set hours ago. Through the open slider between bedroom and porch she could hear the soothing sounds of cicadas and nightingales. The faint scent of wildflowers and the barbecue someone had cooked for dinner lingered in the cool mountain air. "I thought you might want to do something about the rest of the boxes your mother brought us."

She blinked. Sometimes he had the strangest timing. "You're asking me to unpack the rest of our wedding gifts? Now?" When she was just two and a half more days away from having to turn in the biggest proposal of her life?

He shook his head, but gallant as ever, stayed far enough away not to be able to get even a glimpse of the confidential data she was working on. "I'm *asking* if I can move your belongings."

Hadn't they already gone over this at the time they were delivered? "You can't bring them into the living area. Or I won't have room to work. And if we put them in the bedroom—"

He guessed where she was going with this. "We won't have anywhere to sleep."

"Right."

"But if we leave them on the back porch and the storms are even half as fierce as what the weather bureau is predicting, they will get soaked through. That is why I talked to Claire. She said there's room in one of the storage areas behind the party barn, and offered to let us temporarily stash the stuff there for a nominal fee."

Ginger couldn't say she would mind. She had missed being able to sit on the swing on their back porch. Plus, it would be good to take a little break from her work.

She set down her pen and rose. "I'll help you carry them over there."

He put out an arm to block her way. "No. You won't."

Now he was telling her what to do? Trying not to think how long it had been since they had made love, or even really kissed, she propped her hands on her hips. "They're *our* boxes."

"And you're—" At her raised brow, he stopped to censure himself appropriately. "In no condition to be lugging heavy stuff around."

Ginger scoffed. Telling herself that she was glad Rand accepted her continued work and fatigue-related rebuffs, and had not gone all-out to put the moves on her, she joined him on the back porch. Then ambled close enough to whisper, "I'm pregnant, not disabled."

And he, she was pretty sure, was just biding his time. Waiting, the way he always did, until the tension built to the point she couldn't—wouldn't—say no.

Oblivious to the amorous nature of her thoughts, he narrowed his gaze. "You can hold the doors for me. That's it."

Their gazes clashed as strongly as their wills.

"I mean it, Ginger," he persisted in a tone that brooked no dissent.

She thought about arguing. Then wearily gave it up. She could tell this was one battle she wouldn't win.

Aware it felt oddly nice to be fussed over and protected this way—by him—she shrugged as if it did not matter to her either way. "Suit yourself."

He grinned, victorious.

Which in turn made her regret giving in so easily.

But a concession was a concession, so the next fifteen minutes were spent with Rand lugging the collection of wedding gifts outside, while Ginger facilitated his efforts and held the doors open for him. When Rand had fit all the boxes into the bed of his truck, they both climbed into the cab. Rand stretched his arm along the top of her seat as he backed out of the space. "Michelle's office telephoned me today."

Ginger nodded, admitting, "I got a call, too." She just hadn't had the time or inclination to return it.

"They want us to schedule the next appointment so they can get working on the postnup and marriage contract for us." He drove slowly past the Red Sage party barn where a fiftieth wedding anniversary gala was under way.

Trying not to think how happy the partying group looked, or to wonder if and when she would ever have something that incredible to celebrate, Ginger turned her attention forward once again. She did not need to feel wistful.

"When do you want to go?"

Pushing aside her sudden wave of matrimonial loneliness, Ginger looked through the windshield. "When I have time." Why hadn't Rand made more of an effort to get her into his arms again? Usually he was tireless in his pursuit of her. At least when she let him anywhere near her…

He shot her a sidelong glance, seeming to be thinking about a lot more than their current conversation. "Which will be?" With an aggravated frown, he attempted to pin her down.

"I'm not sure. A few weeks maybe." Honestly, she continued, "I really want to get through the Q and A part of the bidding process first." Assuming she made it to the semifinal stage, as she hoped she would.

Rand nodded briefly in understanding. "I'll be too busy to meet with her again until after that's done, too."

Wondering if she should be in more of a hurry to get the postnup done, Ginger fell silent.

Rand parked the truck in front of the door of the storage facility and cut the engine. "Your mother called me."

Uh-oh. Ginger slid out of her seat, circled around to the back and opened the tailgate. "What about?"

Rand loaded boxes onto the dolly he had borrowed from Claire. "Well, first of all, she asked if you were cooking for me."

Ginger stifled a groan. "And what did you tell her?" Nothing, she hoped, that would prompt Cordelia to run right down there and help out again.

Dramatically, Rand parsed his words. "That it was more of a mutual effort, with me grilling…"

"And me pouring prepared salads and cut up fruit into bowls?"

He squinted, thinking. "I *may* have made it sound a lot more labor-intensive than that."

Ginger let loose another mental oath. "She probably didn't believe you."

"She does seem to know you pretty well," he said. Ginger rolled her eyes. So she hadn't exactly been pulling her fair share of the domestic duties. She planned to make it up when he was the one working all the extra hours, vetting the proposals.

They put the first load into the corner of the storage room, then returned for a second.

"What else did my mother say?" Ginger asked curiously.

Strong muscles bunching beneath the smooth cotton fabric of his shirt, Rand lifted several heavy boxes onto the dolly. "She wanted to know why you weren't returning any of her calls."

Ginger tensed, indignant. She defended herself hotly. "I did talk to her, once. And I texted her several times."

"Apparently, that's not good enough to set her mind at ease." Rand angled a thumb at his chest and ventured lightly, "So unless you want *me* playing Twenty Questions with your mom…"

Ginger most certainly did not. She laid a staying hand on his arm. "I'll take care of it."

His muscle warmed beneath her palm, but he made no effort to disengage. Kindly he said, "She sounded worried."

Ginger knew that was true, but that wasn't her fault, either. She turned away from Rand's gentle regard and marched on down the path. "There's no reason to be. My mom knows I'm so swamped with work right now I barely have time to eat and sleep. I also told her I'd call her when I got my bid in."

"Okay, okay." Rand rolled the second load to the storage area. "No need to shoot the messenger."

Ginger winced, aware she had sounded more than a little irritated, and in fact, was moody nearly all the time now. She wanted to say it was all pregnancy hormones, but deep inside, she knew it was more than that. It was loneliness and frustration, yearning and indecisiveness. The need to be with him; the even more fierce need to keep him away. Most of all she worried about falling in love with him, only to have her heart broken—irreparably—later on.

Because the truth was, he hadn't asked for any of this. She was the one who had proposed. She was the one who had needed to be married for business and professional reasons. He was only here because of the baby. Their baby.

And as much as the reckless side of her wanted to see where all this could possibly lead, the honorable side of her refused to trap him into anything other than what they had agreed upon.

"Sorry," she huffed reluctantly.

"Yeah? Well…" He paused next to her, took her chin in hand, and lowered his face to hers, seeming at that moment to have none of her inner ambivalence. "You should be," he teased.

Their eyes met again.

She wanted to tell him to go away even as she ached for him to come even closer. He chuckled wickedly in return. Then his lips pressed against hers in a kiss that was as shockingly intimate as it was unexpected. Sweet, fierce need spiraled through her, arrowing straight from her brain to her heart, to the part of her housing the baby she carried deep inside her.

Ginger moaned, glad he had finally taken the incentive she'd been wishing he would. Yet scared, too. "Damn you," she whispered. "Damn this." *Damn my too vulnerable heart.*

He cupped her face in both hands and brushed his lips over hers. "Damn everything but this," he countered with a smile.

To her regret, another, even steamier clinch followed.

Unable to fight the yearning any more than she was able to resist him, Ginger went up on tiptoe, wound her arms around his shoulders, and brought his lips ever closer. She kissed him again, deeper, slower, more persistently.

He groaned, every inch of him going all hot and hard and male, while she turned soft and feminine and surrendering. His hands slid down to cup the small of her back and fold her tightly against him.

She reveled in his tenderness and the need pouring out of him.

And still he kissed her, again and again and again. Until both of them were panting, trembling for more. And it was only then that Rand pulled back, suddenly in control once again. "As much as I'd like to finish this here and now..." he said roughly.

Ginger knew. They couldn't. Nipples aching, she pulled away from him once again. "Saved by propriety," she quipped with an ease she couldn't begin to feel.

"Temporarily." He walked back to the truck and began unloading what was left. Swiftly. Decisively. One box after another and another...

Ginger used the time to pull herself together and admire the ruggedly beautiful landscape. The thick dark clouds overhead obscured the stars and the moon, and even the rugged mountaintops in the distance. The air seemed to get cooler and damper with every second that passed.

As Rand carried in the last box, big fat raindrops splattered their clothes and the tops of their heads. Hurriedly, they locked up and ran for the truck. They'd hoped to beat the storm, but by the time they got back to their cottage just a few minutes later, rain was falling in thick, heavy sheets.

"I don't have an umbrella so we can either sit here or make a run for it," Rand said from the cab of the truck.

Making a run for it meant getting drenched, head to toe. Waiting it out meant sitting in the truck with the windows steaming up and the rain pounding all around them. And that could only lead to one thing...

Aware she felt far too vulnerable and needy as it was, without bringing sex into the mix once again, Ginger reached for the door handle. In an effort to keep temptation at a minimum, she kept her glance averted. "I don't know about you but I'm making a run for it."

She leaped out into the pouring rain. He was right behind her.

They vaulted into the cottage, clothes plastered to their bodies. Passion pulsed between them, unmet. Ginger sucked in a deep breath. "I'm going to change and then get back to work."

He gave her a long assessing look, knowing what that meant as well as she did. A brief flash of disappointment flickered in his eyes. "Not even a small break?"

Ginger shook her head. As much as she wanted to while away the night in his arms, she couldn't let either of them go down that path. "I still have a lot of proofreading and polishing to do. But I will call Michelle's office tomorrow and get our next appointment set up for the postnup. Because our attorney is right, we do need to get that done." Before their situation got any more complicated than it already was.

Chapter Eight

Eight hours later Rand lay in bed alone, watching the early morning light stream in through the edges of the window blinds. As usual, Ginger had slipped out of bed just before dawn, grabbed a robe and headed for the shower. He remained where he was, fighting the ever-present physical frustration that came with sleeping with but not making love to Ginger.

He shouldn't have been surprised. His wife had said at the outset this was to be strictly for business, a marriage in name only. Like a fool, he hadn't expected the hands-off-each-other dictate to last. But with the exception of their wedding night lovemaking and a few passionate kisses, it had.

The man in him wanted to seduce her right back into his arms. The husband in him knew that would be almost as big a mistake as marrying her on strictly her terms.

The question was, how did he get them out of this quandary without pushing her even further away? He was still searching for a solution when he heard the water shut off. Rustling sounds followed. Then Ginger stepped out of the bathroom, her hair wrapped in a towel, her body clad in a thick knee-length terry-cloth robe, the pajamas she'd been wearing in hand.

Rand watched her go to the suitcases she still refused to

unpack, and rummage through them. Usually, she quickly found what she needed. This time, she didn't, and a soft string of unpleasantries followed.

He smiled, watching her search for the second time. With another beleaguered oath, she stomped over to the bureau where his clothes were stored. Once there, she paused to look hesitantly over her shoulder. He closed his eyes in time to feign continued sleep. Relaxing, she turned her back to him once again, reached into the top drawer and pulled out a pair of his cotton briefs. She nestled them briefly in her hands, appearing to mull over her options, then tiptoed back toward the bathroom.

What was she up to now? Rand didn't know, but he damn sure intended to find out. "Mind telling me where you're going with those?"

A startled Ginger bumped into the wall, then swung back to face him. Rand sat up and switched on the bedside lamp.

They both squinted at the sudden infusion of light. As his eyes adjusted, he saw the pink flooding her cheeks. "I need some clean underwear."

"What's wrong with yours?"

"It's all dirty, and I haven't had time to go to the laundry."

"So you thought you'd wear mine?" he asked wryly.

"It's preferable to going commando, but if you object…"

Imagining that, he grinned.

She heaved an exasperated sigh. "Please tell me you'll let me borrow these just for today."

The thought of her in his boxer briefs brought all sorts of erotic images to mind. "Depends. Can I see you in them?"

She gave me the kind of look a teacher gave a class clown who was acting up. "What do you think?" she retorted.

Best not to go there. "I think we probably should get some laundry done."

Her lower lip shot out. "I'll get around to it as soon as I get my proposal in."

To prevent a stampede all bidders had been given a time slot to hand-deliver their proposals. "How close are you to finishing?"

"We're going to give it one more read-through, and then take it the print shop this afternoon."

"And once that's done?"

She shrugged. "We turn it in and wait."

On pins and needles, it seemed.

She regarded him warily. "When do you and the rest of the panel start the review process?"

"Monday, in the Boernes' attorney's office." Where every drilling plan would be under lock and key, the panel's work under the purview of the managing oil-and-gas attorney, until the semifinal winners were eventually declared.

Ginger groaned and sat on the foot of the bed, his briefs still clutched in her hand. "This whole process is going to take forever."

Breaking down her resistance was what was taking forever.

He caught her by the waist and tugged her toward him. "And there's only one way to make the time go by as quickly as possible." He bussed her temple. "Stay busy together."

"SOMEHOW, THIS WASN'T what I thought you meant this morning," Ginger drawled hours later as the two of them sorted through piles of dirty clothes in the guest ranch laundry. It was after 10:00 p.m., and they were the only two people in the large square room. Which was a good thing, given how many loads they had to do.

"You thought our clothes were going to wash themselves?"

She sent him a droll look.

"Wait." He snapped his fingers as his next idea hit. "You mean you wanted to do this all by yourself? You, being the wife, after all."

Ginger tried not to think how ruggedly handsome he was, with his mahogany hair all rumpled, the shadow of evening beard lining his face. She tossed one of his socks at his head. "You are so funny."

He caught it with one hand. "You mean you want *me* to do it all?"

She dropped her silky delicates into a machine, out of view. "Tempting. But…no."

His gaze roved over her. "Then what do you want?"

Besides the walls between us to stay firmly in place? Ginger wondered. "Us both to do our own laundry," she said firmly.

He sauntered close enough she could smell his brisk, woodsy cologne. "No mingling of the underpants, hmm?"

Warmth climbed from her chest and neck into her face. "Or anything else."

"Easier said than done, given that you're still in my skivvies," he teased.

Her chin lifted. "How do you know?"

"Lucky guess."

His lucky guess was right. A palpable silence fell. She fit her denim jeans into three different machines, and his filled up four. Their shirts went into several more. Her delicates took up yet another machine. His cotton garments the last.

Ginger opened up several rolls of quarters, and together they went down the line, adding money, then detergent and softener. Once all the cycles were selected, they went back to idly roaming the long, brightly lit room. Ginger could tell from the way Rand was looking at her he was thinking about kissing her again. She was wanting, thinking the same. And yet she knew if they succumbed to passion yet again, their marriage would feel like more than a temporary arrangement. And that could be dangerous in so many ways....

Her phone vibrated. Ginger looked at the caller-ID screen, pushed Ignore and put it back in the holder at her waist. "Your mom again?" Rand asked.

"Ex-husband. He's been calling and leaving messages nonstop since he stopped by the other day."

Rand's brow furrowed. "Have you spoken with him?"

"No. Because I know what Conrad wants, and he thinks if he keeps pestering me, he'll get it." She sighed.

"But he won't?"

"Not a chance in this world, no matter what happens next. There's no way I will ever work for him or his father again, and one day soon, he will realize that."

"Good for you," Rand said proudly. He squeezed her hand. "Because you're worth more than the Profitts will ever know."

When he looked at her that way, he certainly made her feel valuable. "Thanks," Ginger whispered.

Rand squeezed her hand again, then let her go.

Regretting the sudden absence of physical contact, Ginger took a seat on one of the plastic chairs next to the windows. The fatigue of a few very long weeks overwhelming her, she closed her eyes and let her head fall back. Stifling a yawn, she felt rather than saw Rand drop down beside her. He slipped an arm around her shoulders and leaned to murmur in her ear, "You know, you can go on back to the cottage and go to bed, if you like. I'll stay and finish here."

Ginger was tempted. Yet, because she knew how much of a slacker she had been on the domestic front since they had married, dutifully protested anyway. "Thanks, but I have to do my jeans my way."

That meant eschewing the dryers and hanging them to dry, so the denim would expand with the weight of the water rather than shrink.

Luckily for them, the bathroom shower rod would support half a dozen of her blue jeans. The Adirondack-style furniture and the swing on the screened-in porch would handle another seven.

By the time they had everything laid out, the clothes in the electric dryers were finished. Ginger helped Rand stuff the clean, warm clothing into plastic baskets and mesh laundry bags. Together, they heaped them into her truck, drove back to their cottage and carried everything inside. Aware it was close to midnight, Ginger yawned again. Rand turned her in the direction of the bedroom. "You're going to bed," he said, the warmth of his hands on her shoulders.

Ginger hated being bossed around, even as she melted at his tender touch. She arched a brow. "Must I remind you that you are not the boss of me?"

He paused. "Must I remind you that you're now sleeping for two? And you have a proposal to turn in tomorrow morning? I presume you want to be fresh and rested for that?"

Ginger wanted to stand her ground. However, her body, her business and the baby nestled deep inside her had other ideas. So, for once, she let her husband call the shots and headed for the bed. Too worn out to look for a clean pair of pajamas, she slipped off her jeans and crawled beneath the covers.

The moment her head hit the pillow, oblivion claimed her.

GINGER WOKE HOURS later to the familiar sound of her mother's voice. "My maternal instinct told me something was wrong!" Cordelia said. "And this mess just proves it!"

"Actually," Rand returned mildly, "the only thing it shows is that neither Ginger nor I are all that great at being domestic."

"Well, someone needs to be, and in most cases, it's the wife!" Cordelia returned.

With a muffled oath, Ginger lifted her head. Unfortunately for her, the door separating the bedroom from the living area was wide open. Catching sight of her, Cordelia swept toward her.

"It's nine o'clock. What are you still doing in bed? Are you feeling all right?"

Ginger sat up in a panic. "I'm supposed to be at the Boernes' attorney's office at eleven!"

"I was just coming in to wake you," Rand said.

"You shouldn't have let me sleep so late." Throwing back the covers, she climbed out of bed and dashed into the bathroom. The jeans hanging on the rod were still pretty wet.

Her mom was right behind her. "What happened here? Were half the dryers all broken? It looks like a laundry room exploded. Not to mention the piles of wrinkled clothing out in the living room."

Ginger followed her mother's glance. It was an apt description.

"I didn't get as far as I might have with the folding," Rand said lamely.

Apparently not. Which would not have mattered had her mother not been here, looking on disapprovingly, her gaze intimating that Ginger was well on the way to botching yet another marriage, due to her lack of domestic instincts.

Trying not to think about how much more the demise

of this relationship was going to hurt than her first one had, Ginger tested the jeans on the back porch. They were nearly as damp as the ones in the bathroom.

The denims she'd had on the day before had a big coffee stain across one thigh. That would have been okay, if she hadn't had an important business meeting to attend.

As intuitive as ever, Rand guessed the direction of her thoughts.

"Want me to toss a pair in the dryer?" he asked.

Ginger hated to accept yet another favor, but had no choice. "If you wouldn't mind, I'd really appreciate it."

"Since when do you line-dry all your jeans?" Cordelia interjected.

"Since I—" *found myself pregnant and unable to fit in practically everything I own* "—married an environmentalist," Ginger said as she searched through the piles of clean wrinkled clothes for two towels.

"Well, I guess that's good for the harmony of the marriage," Cordelia allowed, sniffing as she held up a horribly wrinkled shirt.

Normally, Ginger wouldn't ask, but she was desperate. She turned to her mom. "Do you want to iron something for me?"

Cordelia smiled, happy to be needed. "Absolutely. Afterward, I'll put away the food I brought you."

Ginger rummaged through the piles and plucked out a white knit shirt, and an embroidered cotton vest. "Everything you need, including the spray starch, is in the coat closet. I've got to hit the shower or I'll be late."

Both women sprang to action.

Unfortunately, Ginger's problems didn't end there.

Rand returned with a pair of jeans that was warm and soft—and way too tight. Ginger had to lie on the bed and even then she could hardly shimmy them on. She was still struggling to pull up the zipper when he eased open the door ever so slightly and let himself into the bedroom, ironed clothing in one hand, an oversize stainless-steel travel mug hiding her prenatal vitamins in the other.

"Oh, my heavens," Ginger said, looking at the mug. "Tell me she didn't see."

He whispered in her ear, "Only because I happened to think of it and got there first."

Ginger breathed a huge sigh of relief. "Thank goodness."

Smiling at her tenderly, Rand kept a firm grip on the mug and handed over the ironed garments. "Your mother asked me to bring these to you."

Ginger looked at the clock. It was now ten minutes after ten. She had to leave in seven minutes if she wanted to make it to her appointment on time. Worse, she was beginning to feel vaguely nauseous.

"You look a little green," Rand observed.

Ginger lifted a hand. "Don't say that." To the baby inside her, she whispered, struggling to her feet, "And don't you do this to me!" Not now. Not today...

Rand assisted her the rest of the way to her feet. He looked down at the booty-tight denim. "Are you going to be able to get those snapped?"

Obviously not. She gave him a lethal glare, then took the knit shirt and slipped it over her head. It was as bad as the jeans, showing her burgeoning waistline, and illustrating her inability to snap or fully zip her jeans.

Five minutes left.

Nausea rising.

Ginger took a deep breath, closed her eyes and forced herself to calm down. This shirt wasn't going to work. She went to the closet and selected a tan-colored twill shirt. "Mind if I borrow this?"

"Help yourself."

She slipped it on and put the unbuttoned vest over that. Luckily, the last hole on her belt worked, and it was enough to hold her unzipped pants up on her hips. The oversize man's shirt looked kind of cute, in a tunic-length-shirt sort of way. And it matched nicely with her tapestry-print brown, tan and indigo cotton vest.

She ran a comb quickly through her still-damp copper hair, twisted it into a businesslike knot low on the nape of her neck and slapped her suede cowgirl hat on her head. Grabbing her briefcase, she headed for the door.

"Where are you meeting Maria?" Rand asked.

"In town, outside the lawyer's office."

"Wait—what happened to the shirt I ironed for you?" her mother asked in confusion.

"Wardrobe crisis. Changed my mind!" she replied, and kept right on walking.

"It's some sort of wildcatter superstition." Behind her, Rand explained in his casual, charming tone, "Ginger thinks wearing a piece of my clothing gives her good luck. Who's to say it doesn't?"

Who indeed? Ginger thought.

"I hope it goes well!" her mother rushed to call after her.

"Thanks," Ginger said over her shoulder to both Rand and her mom. The way her day was going thus far, she would need every ounce of luck she could get.

DOT AND CLANCY Boerne were at their attorney's office as the bidders dropped off their proposals. The gregarious couple not only thanked everyone for participating, they took the time to chat a little, as well. With Maria, the focus was on her family and three teenage sons, and what it was like for a woman to manage a mostly male drilling crew.

With Ginger, the focus was the change in her marital status. "So how are things on the home front?" Dot asked.

"Good," she said automatically, a little surprised to realize it was true. Despite the stress of trying to make everything work, she was happier and more content than she had been in a long time. Of course a lot of that could be due to the baby she and Rand were secretly expecting, too.

"Glad to hear that," Clancy said cheerfully.

Dot added, "The first few weeks or months can be harder than anyone expects, due to the adjustments required."

Sensing some reassurance was needed to keep her fledgling company firmly in the running, Ginger said, "Rand and I know that. It's why we've taken a very practical approach to everything on the domestic front."

"Dividing chores evenly, I guess?" Clancy mused.

"Actually, we're trying to keep our lives as close to what they were as possible. Rand and I are very independent at heart. We respect and appreciate that about each other."

Catching Dot and Clancy's look of surprise, Maria grinned and, playfully elbowing Ginger, threw in her two cents. "I've seen the two lovebirds together enough to vouch for that. They're crazy about each other."

Dot smiled approvingly and turned her attention back to Ginger. "The important thing is that you and Rand have realized you belong together and have taken steps to make a lasting commitment to one another, the same way Maria has with her family. That shows a laudable maturity and the kind of personal stability Clancy and I look for in all our business partners."

Meaning what? Ginger wondered, upset. That she wouldn't be in the running if she hadn't married Rand?

Chapter Nine

Ginger was still thinking about the conversation she'd had with the Boernes as she drove back to the Red Sage.

Rand's pickup was gone. So was her mother's sedan. Glad to have a moment alone, she parked and went inside.

The living area of the cottage was pretty much as she'd left it, with unfinished laundry everywhere. The refrigerator, freezer and cupboards were different, however. They were packed with homemade varieties of all her favorite foods. And some of what she now knew were Rand's, as well.

Tears of gratitude blurring her eyes, Ginger reached for her phone. She called her mom to thank her, and this time it was she who got no answer.

She grabbed a couple granola bars and drank a glass of milk. She knew she should start folding and putting away her portion of the laundry, but instead headed right back to bed, shucking her too tight blue jeans as she went.

She climbed beneath the covers, telling herself she'd just rest for a few minutes. The next thing she knew she was waking from one of the soundest, most gratifying slumbers of her life. It was dark outside. Rand was in the living room, sitting on the love seat. But that wasn't the only thing that was different, she noticed as she struggled to sit up. Not by a long shot.

Still yawning and rubbing her eyes, she walked out to join him. Shirttail out, boots off, he looked relaxed and casual.

Noting how the soft blue of his shirt brought out the darker blue of his eyes, she asked, "What time is it?"

He looked at his watch. "Nine o'clock."

That meant she'd been asleep nine hours.

Seeming to realize where her thoughts were going, he patted the seat beside him and said gently, "You were tired."

She certainly must have been. Realizing she was clad in nothing but his shirt—which came to mid-thigh—the unbuttoned vest, and a pair of boot socks, she sat beside him on the small two-cushion sofa and continued to look around at the unusually neat and orderly space. They'd been married for weeks now, and being here with him like this was still a pleasurable assault to her system. "Did you do all this?"

His mouth quirked. "Your mother folded, ironed and organized all our laundry. I assembled the shelving system she insisted we needed. And then we both put everything away."

Ginger blinked in amazement. How was it that he worked so well with her mother while she and Cordelia could barely have a civil conversation these days? "While I was sleeping."

Rand shrugged, as if it was no big deal. His glance fell to her bare thigh, then returned to her eyes. "Your mom knows how to be quiet, as do I."

Her skin tingling where his glance had been, she rose gracefully and walked back into the bedroom. She switched on a light and studied the contents of the closet. It looked the way Ginger's closet had when she was growing up, and her mom had still been in charge of Ginger's life, a fact that was simultaneously comforting and disturbing. Ginger sighed. "She also unpacked my suitcases."

Rand nodded, appearing as relieved about that as her mother probably had been. "Yeah, although given that your toiletries were all in our bathroom and you'd gone through most of the clothing that was in there already, there wasn't a heck of a lot to do there."

Ginger reached for a pair of once loose-fitting but now snug jersey pajama pants and tugged them on over her bare legs. She swung around, feeling trapped and restless once again. "Where are my suitcases?"

Rand draped his arm along the back of the love seat. "With mine, in the storage area, next to the boxes."

"And where's my mom?"

"She was able to get a room at the Summit Inn in town this time. Said she was staying for at least a couple of days."

Days in which, Ginger suspected, the advice on how to live happily married ever after would be free flowing.

Perceptive as ever, Rand leaned forward, hands clasped between his spread knees. "Look, I get that she's a little over-involved, but your mom means well."

Ginger sniffed. "That doesn't make her interference in our home life any easier to take."

Rand moved lithely to his feet and walked toward her. "She said that she wants us to have the best possible start to our marriage. Her way of facilitating that is to create some sort of utopian honeymoon segue into married life. My mom's way is to give us space, and believe me, that's not easy for her."

Ginger walked to the kitchen. Aware she was hungry but didn't yet know what she wanted, she poured herself a glass of milk. "What do you mean?"

Rand slouched against the counter, arms folded in front of him. "In the past, her instinct has always been to rush in and offer her advice whenever she thinks me or my four brothers are making a big mistake. It's caused problems with all of us, in the past. The fact she's not doing it now, coupled with how much your mom is doing, just shows me how much both our families really want our marriage to work."

And that was a problem, too. "I guess I didn't consider the devastation second divorces for each of us would have on our parents."

Abruptly, Rand looked disturbed about that, too.

Sipping her milk, Ginger forced herself to take comfort where she could. "But our families will be happy about the baby, even if they're not happy about our eventual split. And over time, anyway, they're bound to appreciate our commitment to bringing up our baby together, as friends."

FOR RAND, THAT was no longer enough, although it had sounded good at the outset. There was something about living together as a married couple that made them feel like husband and wife, as well. And made him want more from the arrangement than he was currently getting. More sex, more intimacy, more closeness of every kind.

Silence fell between them as Ginger drained her glass and set it aside. Her hair was loose and wild tonight, the rest of her sleep-rumpled and vulnerable. She was heart-stoppingly beautiful to him, and sometimes just looking at her made his chest ache.

Misreading his pensiveness, she went still. "I know you're tempted to shout the news. Sometimes I am, too, but we're not telling anyone yet."

He ran his finger down the curve of her shoulder, and was rewarded with a whole body shudder. "Because of the bid."

Ginger lifted her chin. "I don't want to lose out on this

opportunity because anyone thinks I won't be able to do the work while pregnant."

"They wouldn't necessarily think that." Rand looked at her for a satisfyingly long moment. "My mom worked during all five of her pregnancies right up until the due dates. Any leave she took was after she gave birth."

She inhaled deeply. "She's definitely a role model, and one I intend to emulate. But given what Dot said to me today when I turned in the bid with Maria… I'm not taking any chances."

Ginger filled him in on what had transpired.

Color blooming in her cheeks, she ambled back to the love seat and sank onto it once again. The mountain air streaming in through the open windows was a little chilly, evidenced by the delicious imprint of her nipples against her shirt. She shivered as she glanced over at the stack of papers. "What are you looking at?"

He handed her the folder he'd been perusing when she'd walked in. Ignoring the rigid hardness of his body, he walked over to close the nearest window. He brought a cream-colored fleece throw—another of her mother's homey touches—and draped it across her shoulders. Sinking down beside her, he said, "Those are sales brochures from Summit Realty. Your mom thinks we really ought to consider buying a place."

"That would be the way to go if we planned on being together indefinitely. Since we don't…" Ginger met his eyes and shook her head. "Fiscally, it doesn't make sense. You know that as well as I do."

Rand narrowed his gaze. "Living with a baby in a weekly rental doesn't make sense, either."

Ginger seemed to know they couldn't continue like this. However, to his frustration, that didn't mean she was in any particular rush to figure everything out right this minute, either.

"Can we talk about this later?" Her stomach rumbling, she jumped to her feet and went to the kitchen. "Because I'm starving."

Enjoying the view, he stayed where he was. "At last, something we can agree upon."

She made a soft sound of exasperation, opened the freezer and quickly located one of her mother's homemade meals. "Have you had dinner?" She tossed the words over her shoulder.

"I was waiting for you to wake up."

His shirt rode up slightly in the back, the rumpled hem clinging seductively to the soft jersey covering her buttocks, as she studied the contents of the fridge. "Do you like beef chili?"

I'd rather have you. He let his gaze drift over the delectable, feminine slope of her backside. "So much I can eat it cold out of a can."

Ginger whirled toward him, the curves of her breasts pressing against the cotton fabric of his shirt. "Well, hopefully, we can do better than that."

Hopefully, once dinner was over, they could do a *lot* better than that…

He propped both legs on the coffee table and stretched his arms out along the back of the love seat, content to watch her putter around the small kitchen. Looking pretty and sexy in her usual, determined way, Ginger opened up the fridge once again. She pulled out grated cheddar, sour cream and pickled jalapeños. "What about Frito pie?"

His fingers itched to touch the silky copper hair drifting over her shoulders. "I eat it every chance I get."

"Me, too." Oblivious to how hot and frustrated he was

beginning to feel, Ginger sorted through the dry goods in the cupboards. "Oh, no."

Concerned, he rose and headed toward her. "What's the matter?"

She swung back to him, hands planted on her slender hips. "We don't have any corn chips."

Normally, Rand noted, the lack of any one culinary ingredient was not cause for concern with the woman he'd married. Most of the time, Ginger seemed practically ambivalent about the food she was consuming. But at this particular moment, she looked incredibly distraught. And that could only mean one thing…

He peered at her curiously, both amused and delighted. "Is this your second craving?" The chocolate sandwich cookies with the vanilla cream centers had been her first.

"Don't be silly." Flushing, she waved off the allegation and resumed her determined search of the cupboards. "You know I've been sailing through this pregnancy."

She rummaged around for the travel mug she usually stuck in the very back of the cabinet. Realizing it was time for her to take her prenatal vitamin, Rand held up a staying hand and went to retrieve the bottle hidden in his laptop carrier.

"I also know you've been sipping ginger ale and eating saltine crackers like nobody's business."

He handed her the mug he'd spirited away, and she sent him a grateful look. Probably because his quick thinking that morning had managed to keep her über-organizing mother from finding Ginger's prescription vitamins, thereby preventing her from discovering why it was the two of them had married so hastily.

Ginger shrugged. "They do the trick."

Cocking his head, he studied her for a long moment.

What else had she been holding back from him? "So you *have* been nauseated."

"Just a little bit every now and then. I haven't actually thrown up."

"That's good."

"Tell me about it."

Aware he wanted her to confide more than that in him, he edged near enough to drink in her womanly scent. "Have you had any other cravings?"

She filled a glass with milk, stirred in a little chocolate syrup and swallowed a prenatal vitamin. "I never said this was one."

He folded his arms. Waited.

And was rewarded with a blush and an almost smile. She lifted both her hands in grudging self-defense. "Okay, if it will make you happy, yes! I *have* been wanting Frito pie made with my mom's chili for weeks now." She shrugged off his amused laugh and bent to find a saucepan in the cupboard. "But that happens to me anyway when I've gone too long without some really fine home cooking. It happens to everyone."

She paused to dump the frozen block of homemade chili in the saucepan, and set it on the stove. "That's why the subliminal messaging in TV food commercials is so successful." She turned the burner on medium heat, then put on the lid, and pivoted back to him. "Once you see a hamburger with everything, you can't rest until you actually have one."

Leaning close, he ran a thumb over her cheek and needled her playfully, "If you *like* hamburgers. I don't imagine the messaging works on you if you don't."

She grinned at his teasing, the way she always did, and tilted her face up to his. "You know what I mean. Furthermore—" she jabbed her thumb at the valley between her soft, luscious breasts "—*I'd* be perfectly happy eating our chili without anything but cheddar cheese and sour cream and jalapeños."

Except she wouldn't, Rand thought, when she'd had her heart set on Frito pie. And they both knew it. Ginger was the kind of woman who wanted *what* she wanted *when* she wanted it. Just like he wanted what he wanted—which, at the moment, was mostly…her.

Oblivious to the licentious direction of his thoughts, she looked at the clock, realizing, as did he, that the grocery stores in the area were all closed until morning. She scowled. "Do not make me feel silly about this."

"Wouldn't think of it." Aware this was one problem he could actually solve, he headed for the door.

"Where are you going?" He tempted her with an easy grin, admiring anew the way his shirt gently outlined her breasts. The changes in her body were subtle but incredibly erotic. "Off to save the day, of course."

RAND WAS BACK fifteen minutes later, grinning as though he had just won the lottery, two single-serving packages of Fritos in hand.

Ginger tore her glance from the handsome contours of his face, and pretended to be busy at the stove. "Where'd you go?"

He sauntered closer, with exaggerated chivalry. "My mom's cottage. She didn't have any Fritos, unfortunately, nor did any of the other guests in adjacent cottages."

Mortified that he'd been reduced to begging for corn chips at ten-thirty at night, Ginger covered her face with her hand. "Tell me you're kidding me."

He shifted even closer, his voice low and sexy. "I kid you not." She peered at him through spread fingers, aware she had never been this fussed over by any man. "So who *did* have them?"

"Heath and Claire."

The proprietors of the Red Sage guest ranch.

He slouched against the counter next to her, legs crossed at the ankle, hands on either side of him. "I figured they've got kids in elementary who take lunches to school. And what goes better with sandwiches and fruit than chips? So seeing their lights were still on downstairs, I went over to the main house and explained the situation—"

Ginger tore her gaze from his rock-solid chest and abs. "You told them that I was—"

He lifted a hand to her face, gently touching her cheek, and flashed her a crooked smile. "Celebrating the completion of one of your work deadlines. We were all set for Frito pie, only to find out we were fresh out of corn chips. They were happy to give me what they had, although they refused to take cash for it, so we'll have to replenish their stock tomorrow."

Ginger paused, still not sure whether she wanted to kiss or scold him. And still the chili bubbled on, filling the cottage with its fragrant spicy smell.

Aware she was still tingling from his brief sensual touch, she took a deep breath. "You're sure they didn't guess we were expecting?"

Rand shrugged and wrapped his arm around her shoulders. "They didn't appear to."

"Or worse, think we were being ridiculous?"

He kissed her temple, cheerful as ever. "We are newlyweds."

"Newlywed professionals in our early thirties," Ginger corrected, telling herself not to read anything into the easy affection in his eyes. "Who should be beyond such silliness."

Rand paused thoughtfully. "What's the real problem here?"

"I just don't want to appear frivolous when I'm trying so hard to get people to take me seriously."

"First of all," he said, taking down two stoneware bowls from the cabinet, "no one who knows you thinks you are the least bit ditzy, on any level." He opened up two packets of chips, and poured them into the bottom of each bowl, then ladled a generous amount of beef chili over top. "Everyone knows how serious and hardworking you are in every respect. But you're still entitled to enjoy yourself."

Aware if she were truthful, there was only one way she really wanted to enjoy herself—in his arms, in their bed— Ginger added a healthy sprinkling of cheddar, some fresh chopped tomato, several jalapeño slices and a dollop of sour cream to the fare. "Believe me, I wish I could spend a lot more time having fun than I have lately."

But Ginger wasn't sure even that was a good idea.

THEY CARRIED THEIR dinner out onto the back porch and sat side by side on the porch swing. The evening was breezy and cool, with a full moon and stars shining above. Enjoying the time alone with his wife, Rand slanted her a curious glance. "If you want to have more fun, why don't you take more time to relax?"

Ginger carefully gathered all the ingredients on her spoon. She lifted the steamy concoction to her lips, blew lightly across the top. For a moment she savored the incredible mix of flavor and texture. Rand did the same. From the look on his face, he found the dish as deliciously satisfying as she did.

Finally she allowed, "I can't afford to goof off when I have so much riding on the drilling rights to this particular oil lease."

"Maybe too much," Rand decreed candidly, reminding her with a frown that as important and potentially lucrative as the Boerne lease was, securing it was just *one* job.

There would certainly be other opportunities down the line.

"Since you've only really pursued the one property here, why not start vying for leases in some of the other up-and-coming areas, outside of Marfa or Fort Stockton—where I don't already have contracts to do the environmental screening—from here on out?" Where there would be no conflict of interest between them? Or her and his mother's company, for that matter?

"If you want to work in those areas, I give you my word that I won't," Rand assured her. "And in the interest of family harmony, I'll get my mother's company to avoid bidding in that area, too."

Her expression both reflective and conflicted, Ginger ate a little more, then took a sip of her milk. "I can't afford to do that."

"Why not?"

She raked her spoon through the center of her chili, mixing the melted cheddar and sour cream. Finally she muttered, "I guess it's not as if you won't find out soon enough anyway." She pushed a jalapeño pepper to the side, took another bite, sighed. "I have enough money in the trust fund I got from my dad to pay Maria and her drilling crew to work under my direction for thirty days, but that's it." Her lips flattened. "We either get a viable flow out of the shale deposits the first time out, or I'm done here."

"Maria's company couldn't pick up the slack?"

"She's on as much of a shoestring budget as I am. And she has a weekly payroll to meet. She can only afford to work for jobs and people that pay as they go."

"So you're stuck. This one job, and that's it."

"Yep."

Taking a long swallow of beer, he studied her quietly. She looked stressed and worried again, none of which was any better for their baby than it was for her. "And it has to be the Boerne lease?" Where the competition was exceptionally fierce. "No other property in the area will do?"

She inhaled deeply. "The satellite imagery, soil samples, and even the 'creekology' or lay of the creek beds on the Boerne land are all incredibly positive. I've walked that ranch. I can't explain it except to say that I know in my gut that particular strata of rock is going to produce vast amounts of oil. The other properties in this area might or might not."

Rand's mother and grandfather had the same innate talent for scouting out the big energy fields. It was a God-given sixth sense few had, and all wanted. If Ginger had it, too, she was more like his wildcatter family than she realized.

"The challenge will be to get the oil out safely," she continued soberly, "with as little disruption and damage as possible to the existing ranch."

Rand knew Ginger was talented enough to do that, too. The big question was, who would the Boernes select? And how would Ginger react if all she had done thus far was for naught? Would she renege on what she'd said so far, take her ex up on his offer and go back to work for Profitt Oil?

Ginger put her empty dish aside. Shivering in the damp evening air, she curled up next to him on the swing. "I've spent months courting Dot and Clancy. I've thrown all my research and testing budget at this one project. I don't have enough money to start all over again. If I don't land this bid with the Boernes, then I'm going to have to call it quits and go back to working for someone else again."

Rand put his dishes aside, too. He sat back, wrapped

an arm around her shoulders and pulled her into the curve of his body. He leaned over and pressed a tender kiss on the top of her head. "And you don't want to do that," he ventured.

Ginger continued staring stubbornly at the shield of trees on the other side of the screen. "I want the freedom to pick the jobs that are right for me. And our child. The only way I'll really be able to do that is if I'm my own boss."

Another silence fell.

Rand inhaled the familiar soap and shampoo scent of her hair and skin. "Then I hope, at the end of the day, the Boernes pick you."

Ginger tilted her head to look at him. Wistfulness and something else he couldn't quite read gleamed in her pretty green eyes. "You mean that," she acknowledged softly.

Rand nodded. "I've already got plenty of work in Summit County. If you're awarded this lease, more will follow. That would be good for you, good for our baby, good for us." He threaded his hand through her hair. "And speaking of that, you know what else would be good for us?"

Ginger caught her breath. "I have a feeling you're going to show me."

It was all the invitation Rand needed. "You're right. I am."

Chapter Ten

Rand shifted Ginger over onto his lap, so she was straddling him, and then pivoted himself to the center of the swing. Hardly believing how good she felt against him, her breasts pressed against his chest, her inner thighs cupping the outside of his, he tipped her face up to his and kissed her long and wet and deep. Kissed her until she fisted both hands in his hair and quivered. "Rand." She whimpered for more as he slid his hands beneath her shirt, ghosted lovingly over her ribs. "What are you doing?"

He found what he was looking for, the soft, warm swell of breasts, the hard jut of her nipples pressing against the center of his palm. She moaned again at the erotic sensations he dispensed, grinding against him.

Chuckling affectionately, he went on a little tour, kissing, unbuttoning and unfastening. Until her shirt was off, and then so was her bra. And God help him if she wasn't the most beautiful woman he had ever seen in his entire life.

He bent his head to kiss the tight, puckered tip. Savored the moment as she caught his head in both her hands and held it there. Taking her nipple into his mouth, he quipped, "I'm helping you have a little fun."

Her head was back, her eyes closed, as he worshiped one breast, then the other. She moaned again when he eased a hand beneath the waistband of her pants and found the most feminine part of her. "This isn't fun," she gasped, her hips rocking helplessly. "It's sex." Eyes still closed, she shivered in delight, still having enough moxie to protest, "Which happens to be what got us into trouble in the first place!"

Rand recalled all too well the recreational activities they had shared on Valentine's Day. And the satisfying surrender that had followed… Memories that fueled his fantasies to this day.

Gripping her hips in the way he knew she really liked, he moved her back and forth across his lap, kissing her passionately until she writhed with pleasure and kissed him back. Finally, when she was soft and warm and eager, he lifted his head long enough to stare into her eyes. "I don't know about you, but I kind of like the trouble we're in."

She didn't respond…she didn't have to. He could see how she felt even if she wouldn't yet actually say so.

Shifting her off his lap, and onto the center of the swing, he dropped to his knees. Her green eyes softened all the more and her breath caught as he stripped the rest of her bare and tenderly worshiped the quivering inner skin of her thighs, her navel.

Another moan wrenched from her lips. "Spoken like a man."

Determined to make her concede it was foolish to stay away from each other physically, the way they had been trying to do, he left a trail of kisses over her lower abdomen, her silky-wet center. Aware he wanted every part of her, he murmured, "You can fib all you want, but I know you want me, too."

She leaned forward, took his head in her hands and kissed him back in the way he'd been wishing for. "How?" she demanded, stubborn as ever.

"By this." He touched her erect nipples. Moved lower still, to the dampness between her thighs. "And this." He moved his fingers in the way she liked, until she pulsated. "And this."

"So I'm weak…" She arched against him pliantly, still kissing him. "At least," she whispered, "where you're concerned…"

He moved her hand to the proof of his desire, wanting, needing her to feel what she did to him, too. "Then that makes two of us," he told her gruffly, "because I can't resist you, either.…"

Ginger knew she could have let Rand possess her then. They would have both climaxed, and could have called it a night. But she didn't want it to be over, didn't want him having all the fun. All the control. So she stripped him naked, too. Made him take a turn on the swing while she found new and inventive ways to pleasure him. And only when he put his hands beneath her bottom and tugged her to him, did she straddle him again. Only when he kissed her with the passion that had been so sorely missing from their married life, did he fill her with one smooth stroke, pressing into her with such perfection that she cried out from the sheer pleasure of it. Only then did she let him send her spiraling again, and only then, when she was at the pinnacle of desire, did he follow.

To their mutual pleasure, the aftershocks were as potent as their lovemaking had been. Letting them know that once again they had risked it all. Just to be together again.

Trembling, Ginger clung to Rand.

She couldn't believe she had done this. Again. Let her heart get miles ahead of her head, let them risk such disappointment. But she had. Worse, she wasn't sure what she was going to do about it.

Because getting this close to each other—and they were becoming more enraptured with every passing moment— was not part of their original agreement.

GINGER WAS STILL in bed the next morning, nibbling on a saltine and taking long slow breaths in through her nose and releasing out through her mouth, when Rand strolled in.

As usual, he had hit the complimentary daily breakfast buffet at the main house, and had thoughtfully brought something back for her. This morning, it was spinach and artichoke quiche, fruit compote and a decaf latte. He set the repast on the night table beside her bed.

The aroma, pleasant as it was, sent her severely challenged equilibrium even closer to the edge.

Looking sexy as ever in a T-shirt and jeans, Rand sat on the edge of their bed. "Your mom called. She wants us to have dinner with her this evening."

Reminding herself that she had successfully battled the malady thus far, Ginger struggled to contain her nausea. "Just us, or is your mom invited, too?"

"It'll be the four of us."

She wiped a bead of sweat from her temple. "This is starting to be a regular thing. Although I'm not so sure it's a good thing."

Her mother was too nosey; his mom too observant and astute.

He grinned in agreement and offered her a hand. The moment Ginger sat all the way up she knew she was in trouble. She shoved him out of the way and, hand to her mouth, ran for the bathroom.

By the time she finished, tears were streaming from her eyes. Afraid to venture too far from the commode, she sank down on the cool tile. Rand knelt beside her. He placed a cold wet towel on the back of her neck, and handed her another for her face.

"So much for jalapeños," Ginger joked weakly in an effort to cover her humiliation.

He shoved the damp hair from her forehead, agreeing gently, "So much for morning sickness…."

Amen to that, Ginger thought. What a horrible way to start the day.

He slid her another tender look, then rose and returned a second later with a glass of ice water and lemon slices. "That's supposed to help."

"Reading up again?" She took a cautious sip.

He gently helped her to her feet. "I like to be prepared for whatever comes my way. And since you admitted you'd been feeling nauseated the last few weeks…"

Ginger paused at the sink to brush her teeth and rinse with a mint-flavored mouthwash. With his arm around her waist, she made her way back to bed. She sank onto the rumpled sheets, wishing she hadn't just disgraced herself in front of him. Talk about sexy…

She was glad he was there anyway. Just having him near made her feel better. She let her gaze drift over every ruggedly handsome inch of him. "You're too gallant for your own good. You know that?"

The faint hint of a smile curved of his lips. "What can I say?" He covered the back of her hand with his. "It's a family trait all the McCabe men share." His grip was warm and comforting. Sighing inwardly, Ginger turned her palm over, so she could hold on to him.

The moment drew out.

Another inscrutable look. A tantalizing grin.

Her nipples peaked. "You can't possibly be thinking what I think you're thinking," she accused.

But he was.

"See?" His voice was low and a little rough. He kissed the back of her hand, the inside of her wrist. "I'm not so gentlemanly, after all. Especially when this is one of our rare mutual days off." He worked his way up to her elbow.

"Besides, what better way to get that newlywed glow going before we see the two moms?"

She stared down at the sight of his lips on her skin. Their lovemaking the night before had been enough to have her falling in love with him. Another bout might make it last forever.

And the vows that bound them together were not the everlasting kind.

Determined to protect both of them, from as much hurt and disappointment as possible, Ginger curled a hand around his biceps. "Actually, there is something else that needs to be done before we see our mothers."

Intrigued, he lifted a brow and gestured for her to continue.

"We need to finish drawing up the terms of our marriage contract." It was only half done and at this rate, they'd never be ready for their next meeting with the family law attorney.

Her suggestion had the effect of a bucket of cold water poured over his head. His expression went from playful to recalcitrant, just like that. "You really want to do that today?" Before they ended up making love again?

"Yes, I do. So...." Resolutely, she tossed back the covers, went to the fridge, came back with their half-finished list and a pen. "Let's get started."

"WHAT HAVE THE two of you been doing today?" Cordelia asked when Rand and Ginger met up with the two moms at the Summit Inn.

"Working on our postnup," Ginger said.

Cordelia and Josie exchanged glances rife with maternal concern.

Not wanting to get into that again, Ginger asked the moms the same question.

Josie said, "Preparing for the Q and A session with the Boernes. I know we haven't won anything yet—"

But she expected her company to win. Ginger expected Wyatt Drilling to make it to the semifinals, too. Everyone did.

"It just makes sense to be prepared," his mom finished.

Abruptly, Ginger wondered if she should have been doing the same instead of just waiting around for the announcement. She hadn't been worried about the Q and A; to date, she'd spent so long engineering her oil-recovery plan she knew the facts of her proposal inside and out. Maria was equally prepared to discuss the actual drilling process.

Ready to learn from one of the best, however, since she now had access to Texas's most famous lady wildcatter, Ginger looked at Josie. "If you don't mind my asking, how do you get ready for that?"

"I have someone on my team grill me."

Ginger's mom looked at her. "I could do that for you," Cordelia offered.

"That would be fine, Mom. But I really need to get someone who knows the ins and outs of oil exploration. Like Maria, my drilling partner."

"Oh." Cordelia briefly looked hurt. Her next idea hit just as suddenly. "Rand can't do it?" she asked with all the tenacity of a veteran helicopter mom.

Ginger shook her head. "There's a firewall between us. We can't discuss the bids."

Josie conceded, "I can't help her, either, since my company is competing against hers."

Cordelia turned back to her daughter. "Maybe you should take this as a sign, then, and just drop out."

"No!" Rand, Ginger and Josie all said in unison.

Ginger knew her mom meant well; that didn't necessarily help. "I've gone too far for that, Mom," she explained with as much patience as she could muster. "Now, what did you want to tell us this evening?"

"Actually, it's what I'd like to show you. So if you don't mind coming along for the ride—" Cordelia ushered them all into her Cadillac.

"I have to tell you, I have really fallen in love with this little town," Cordelia said as she drove to a Craftsman-style home on Oak Street.

Ginger immediately recognized it as one of the homes in the Realtor brochures Rand had been perusing the evening before. Except now there was a "sold" sticker across the front of the yard sign.

Cordelia parked in the driveway and got out. "Let's go in, shall we?"

Ginger had a sinking feeling. "Mom." Ignoring Rand and Josie McCabe's perplexed expressions, she dug in her heels. "What did you do?"

Cordelia waved her hand dismissively. "I want you to see the inside first."

Feeling a migraine coming on, Ginger pressed her hands to her head. "Tell me you didn't buy this for us as some sort of an over-the-top wedding gift."

Cordelia affirmed, "I didn't buy it for you."

Ginger's whole body sagged in relief.

The older woman turned the key in the lock and opened the door onto one of the nicest interiors Ginger had ever seen. She turned with a smile, announcing, "I bought it for me."

RAND HAD NO idea what to say. Nor, if their expressions were any indication, did his mother or his wife.

"You bought this home," Josie repeated to Cordelia, as if saying the words out loud would somehow shed light on the situation.

Cordelia walked through the spacious, well-lit rooms. "Initially, I wanted a place to stay when I'm in town, visiting." She turned, admiring the sunny yellow walls and gleaming wood floors. "Then I thought about how far the drive was between San Angelo and Summit, a good four hours under the best of circumstances, sometimes a lot more. And the fact that there are no easy commuter flights between the two places. So I decided I would move here instead."

Ginger stared at her mother, all the color draining from her face. "Tell me you didn't quit your job."

"I quit my job."

Josie's hand flew to her heart.

At least his mom knew what a mistake this was, Rand thought wryly.

"But only because I got one here," a beaming Cordelia continued.

"Where?"

"With Claire McPherson—at the Red Sage guest ranch."

Coincidentally, Rand thought, where he and Ginger were now living.

"Apparently, they're short-staffed for events in their party barn. And with the busy summer season coming up, she was delighted to have me on board."

Ginger slumped down on the staircase. She looked so wobbly, Rand sat beside her and put his arm around her.

"What about your house in San Angelo?" she asked.

Cordelia shrugged. "I put it on the market. Since it's in such good shape and I priced it reasonably, it won't take long to sell."

An uncomfortable silence fell.

Ginger stared at her mother in abject misery. "You realize I haven't actually won any work here yet, Mom."

Unperturbed, Cordelia walked over to a window and

adjusted the shade, so even more light poured into the room. "You will, honey. But even if you don't, it's my understanding that Rand has plenty of work."

Ginger stiffened and got to her feet. "What does that have to do with me?"

It was Cordelia's turn to look annoyed. She sent her only child a chastising look. "Plenty, since you're his wife, and part of being his spouse is creating a warm and loving home for him."

Rand rose. He hated to be in the middle of this, but since his name had been mentioned, he had no choice. "Ginger's been doing fine on that score," he said easily.

"Really?" Cordelia spun toward him. "You forget. I've seen the way the two of you have been living."

Ginger huffed. "So?"

Cordelia stepped forward, her hands knotted at her sides. "How many home-cooked meals has she prepared for the two of you? Has she prepared even one?"

Rand nodded, making no effort to disguise his pleasure. "We had chili with all the fixin's last night," he announced.

"Chili that I made and brought to you," Cordelia corrected. "Had I not…"

"Food isn't the issue here," Josie interrupted her.

Cordelia sniffed and folded her arms in front of her. "Really? I beg to differ."

"Rand and Ginger's privacy is," Josie asserted.

The two mothers-in-law stared at each other in stony silence.

"And to that end—" Rand interjected.

"I think everyone should back off," Ginger put in. Her expression distraught, she headed blindly for the door.

"Believe me, I would—" Cordelia cut her off at the threshold "—if I thought you were coming even close to meeting your husband's needs. Don't you see? Your marriage to Rand will fail as surely as your first failed, if you don't put your husband first!"

Rand wrapped his arms around his wife's shoulders. "Our marriage will fail if we don't put each other first," he corrected her. Able to see Ginger was at her limit, which in his view was understandable, he continued mildly, "And to that end, I think Ginger and I should take a rain check on dinner this evening."

Sagging with relief, Rand's mother quickly added, "Actually, I'm feeling rather tired, too."

Cordelia glared at Josie in disbelief. "You're siding with them?"

The lady wildcatter shrugged her shoulders in abject surrender. "I'm not siding with anyone. I'm just saying we all need a time-out."

"Amen to that," Ginger muttered beneath her breath.

They all looked at each other. It seemed everyone was in agreement except Cordelia. "I'll drive you back, then," she said stiffly. She ushered everyone outside onto the front porch and locked the door behind them.

The two older women headed for the car, but Ginger hung back. "Rand and I are going to walk."

Cordelia started to argue, then stopped. "Suit yourself," she said. Face rigid with hurt and disapproval, she got in the car with Josie and drove off.

Silence fell between Rand and Ginger. He was glad his wife had opted to walk back to their vehicle, which was still parked at the Summit Inn. They needed time alone. It was a pleasant spring evening. And the distance wasn't all that far.

Ginger raked her hands through her hair. She shook her head in disbelief. "What a nightmare."

Rand took her hand in his, gave it a reassuring squeeze. "I guess you weren't kidding when you said your mom was a helicopter parent. Up to now, I thought it was kind of cute, the way she kept butting in, trying to help."

Her eyes glittered with frustration. "And now?"

He shrugged. "Frankly, it's a little scary, realizing she could drop everything to follow us to a job site."

Ginger leaned into Rand's touch. "She pulled herself together once, when she reacted like this, after my dad died. I'm sure she can do it again."

Figuring she needed more than simple hand-holding, Rand tugged her against his chest and wrapped his arms around her. "And in the meantime?" he asked, feeling the rapid beat of her heart.

Ginger blew out a weary breath and turned tortured eyes up to his. "We brace ourselves for even more interference."

How are you doing?" Josie asked Rand several days later when she ran into him outside city hall.

"Okay," he said. Given the fact he had been locked in the Boernes' attorney's office for at least twelve hours every day with the other members of the independent review board, evaluating all the proposals and red-flagging any potential problems, for the upcoming Q and A sessions.

"And Ginger? How has she been?"

Not as well, Rand admitted silently. She was on pins and needles as she waited to find out whether she would advance to the semifinal round or be eliminated. But he figured his mom knew that.

"Are she and Cordelia still on the outs?" Josie prodded.

"Pretty much, yeah."

Josie waited, sensing there was more. Needing to unburden himself to someone, Rand continued, "The day after Cordelia told us about the move to Summit, she came over to the cottage to apologize."

Josie paused. "What's wrong with that?"

Rand rubbed at the tense muscles in the back of his neck. "Cordelia also dropped off a binder of favorite family recipes."

His mom winced. "Let me guess. Ginger hasn't been near a stove since."

He nodded. "Not that this is necessarily a problem except that Ginger hasn't wanted *me* to cook anything for us, either. Instead she asks me to bring takeout for both of us every night on my way back from town."

Rand had humored Ginger, like countless expectant dads before him, because she was hormonal and totally stressed out. However, the "not cooking anything on principle" was beginning to get old. Especially when they had a freezer full of homemade dinners.

Rand studied his mom. "You understand where Ginger is coming from, don't you?"

Josie nodded. "This is a very tough business to break into, for anyone."

Rand remembered that little bit of family history. "But you made it happen anyway."

"Over both my parents' objections, since my dad thought the oil business was no place for a woman and my mother wanted me to be part of Dallas society."

Rand smiled, still not really able to envision his tomboy mother making her official debut to the social elite in a white gown and gloves, although he had seen the photos that proved she had indeed endured what she had considered the ultimate in public humiliation. "You quit that, too."

"Not until after my debutante years." Josie sighed. "And not without enduring a lot of quarreling with both my parents. Ginger is a strong, smart, independent woman, Rand. She'll figure out a way to handle Cordelia, same as you and you brothers have all found ways to deal with me when I've meddled in your lives."

Rand was glad his mother had finally backed off. It helped, not having to bicker with her, too. It also helped being able to come to her with his problems, at least when it came to understanding women. "What should I do in the meantime?"

"Be there for Ginger. But don't, under any conditions, try to tell her what to do."

That, Rand already knew. "And when it comes to Cordelia?"

Josie paused, thinking. "I'm not sure how successful I'll be, but I'll try to get Cordelia to ease up a little."

"I'd appreciate it. Ginger's got enough on her plate right now without dealing with her mom's disapproval."

Josie started to say something, then stopped. She gave him an odd look, but still didn't say what was on her mind. Finally she asked instead, "How is Ginger's preparation going for the Q and A sessions?"

Rand tensed. "She won't say." But Rand had a feeling, given the way his new wife had been walking around the cottage, scowling and muttering to herself when she and Maria weren't rehearsing together, not all that well.

Finally he admitted, "I'm trying to give Ginger the space she needs."

Josie nodded approvingly. "I'm sure she appreciates it."

Did she? It was hard to tell. All Rand knew for certain was that Cordelia's criticism of her daughter's ability to participate in an effective marriage had put a damper on his relationship with Ginger. He wasn't sure how to get them back on solid footing. He only knew that it wouldn't happen until Ginger found out whether she had won—or lost—the biggest business opportunity of her life.

WHEN RAND WALKED in Monday evening Ginger was going through all the line-dried denim in her closet. He had missed her, during the hours he had been around, but there was no telling from her expression whether or not she had missed him.

Glad to be home again, nevertheless, he went to her side, watching as she tersely checked out one label, then another, and another. "Wardrobe crisis?"

Her lips twisted unhappily. "Something like that."

The shirt she had borrowed from him clearly wasn't the problem. She looked pretty and ultra-casual in the oversize light green button-up.

In no hurry to go anywhere, he lounged against the bureau, arms crossed at his chest. Steadfastly ignoring his presence, she shucked off the pair of paisley pajama pants she'd been wearing and pulled on a pair of denim. To her visible frustration, there was no way they would come even close to zipping. With a muttered oath, she took off the pants and tried another pair to the same result.

"Maybe you should buy some maternity clothes," Rand offered casually.

She sent him an irascible look and shook her head. "It's way too soon for that."

Rand didn't really see what the big deal was. Yes, her waistline was thickening, but only because their baby was growing inside her.

Ginger sat on the edge of the bed, the long tails of his shirt covering her bare thighs. "I am going to have to buy larger clothes, though."

"Want me to go with you?"

She flashed him a droll look. "To do what? Hold my purse?"

Rand shrugged. "Or get sizes for you, or whatever."

Not above doing what had to be done to get to spend more time with her, and perhaps regain some of their previous closeness and make love again, Rand used what leverage he had. "If you want people to think our relationship is as authentic as our skills in the field, we're going to have to be seen together at least some of the time. Otherwise, people are going to start to wonder what's going on with us."

That got her. "Okay, fine." Ginger vaulted to her feet and put on a pair of sexy black yoga pants with a roll top that ended several inches below her navel. "As long as we get dinner in town before we come back here."

Rand shrugged. "Fine with me." He could use a good meal and some quality time with his new bride.

Together, they headed for Summit, and once there, went straight to Callahan Mercantile & Feed, an old-fashioned general store that carried everything from camping gear to authentic Western wear.

Rand accompanied her inside. "So what are you looking for?"

She headed for the shelves of ladies' jeans and plucked up several different sizes. "Loose-fitting, practical work clothes." She handed him a stack of different styles and sizes, then moved on to the cotton vests and men's twill shirts. Satisfied she had enough to try on, she found a unisex fitting room located in the middle of the clothing area. The look in her eyes said she did not want him to come in with her, so he waited outside the locked door.

And then waited. And waited. And waited.

Wondering what was going on in there, and hoping she wasn't starting to feel sick again, he moved closer. "Ginger? Everything okay in there?" No answer. "Honey?" he prompted, a little louder.

Hannah Callahan Daugherty, the proprietress of the mercantile, appeared at his side. Married and a mother herself, the slender brunette flashed an easy-going smile. "How's it going?"

Rand wished to heck he knew. "I'm a little concerned about my wife," he confessed.

A huff sounded from behind solid oak. "Oh, for heaven's sake!" The dressing room door slid open slightly and Ginger reached for him. "Just come in," she ordered, exasperated.

Mindful of the soft, feminine hand suddenly fisted in his shirtfront, Rand shrugged good-naturedly. "Women!"

Hannah laughed and moved off. "Just let me know if you need anything," she said over her shoulder.

Ginger tugged Rand the rest of the way inside. As he had feared, her eyes were red and glistening with tears. "Must you make everything such a big deal?" she snapped. He wasn't the one who had locked himself in here, crying.

"What's the problem?" he asked quietly, as calm as she was emotional.

She plucked at the sides of her jeans, which seemed to comfortably fit her thickening waistline but overwhelm everything else. Her lower lip trembling, she whispered back, "I look like I'm wearing jodhpurs, that's what. But I can't go down a size, because if I do, they won't fit me in the waist and I won't be able to get them zipped."

Rand eyed the pile of discarded garments. It certainly seemed as though she had been busy while he'd cooled his heels. "What about the other styles?"

Ginger threw up her hands. "They're even worse. I either can't get them on…or I can and the tummy on them sticks out a mile, making me look a lot more—" She gestured comically as if outlining the belly of a whale. "Than I already am," she finished finally.

Rand knew when he was in over his head. "Want me to call Hannah in?" Surely the storekeeper would know how to get a better fit.

"No!"

He leaned close enough to her ear, then dared ask, "Want me to take you to a maternity store up in Fort Stockton?"

Her glare turned lethal. "How do you know where the closest one is?"

Damn, she was pretty when she was agitated. He shrugged. "Same as always. I researched it online." He paused to smooth a lock of silky copper hair from her face. Tenderly, he tucked it behind her ear, then murmured, "You could always order something off the internet."

"There's no time for that. I have to find something to wear right now, that I won't look ridiculous in." Moisture flooded her green eyes. She dashed away her tears with her knuckles, before they could fall.

He tried to simultaneously problem-solve and tease her out of her dejected mood. "You could borrow a pair of my jeans, the same way you do my shirts. Because those probably would work, since they're just sort of straight up and down." He illustrated with his hands. "Instead of all nipped in or curvy."

It had been a shot in the dark, born of sheer desperation.

Ginger's eyes lit up.

She let out a low, delighted laugh and palmed the center of his chest. "Out of the mouths of the unenlightened," she blurted.

Grabbing her phone, she quickly looked up the measurements on the pants she'd been wearing. He helped her convert them to men's sizing.

An hour later they left the store. Ginger had half a dozen pairs of men's jeans, a few men's shirts and a couple new ladies' vests—in a larger size, to accommodate her blossoming breasts—bundled together in a mercantile shopping bag.

She was wearing a new pair of men's jeans, too. "Feel

better now?" Rand asked, winding a protective arm around her waist.

Ginger leaned into him briefly, looking happier and more relaxed than he had seen her in days. "Much. I should have gone for the 'Southwestern' Annie Hall slash Katherine Hepburn style of dressing much earlier."

He tucked her in closer to his side, predicting, "You'll have people talking."

"But it will be about why I'm suddenly electing to wear all men's clothing."

Her triumph was as much an aphrodisiac as her temper. In fact, everything about her got his engine running.

"And you'll say…?"

She winked. "That I would have done it a whole lot sooner if I had only known how much more comfortable guy's clothes were than gal's."

Rand grinned, glad she had solved her problem, and would be able to get through the next few weeks, or months, comfortably. Playfully he tweaked her nose. "So, back to the dinner you promised me…" His stomach was growling hungrily. As was hers.

She slanted him her usual feisty look. "We're having pizza. And I'm paying."

"Works for me." Matter of fact, anytime he was with her, anywhere he was with her, worked for him.

They paused to lock her new clothes in his pickup, then walked down Main Street. They were nearly to Salvio's Pizza Place when they saw Maria standing in front of the fire station, where her truck was parked. Conrad was standing next to her, and they were talking. It didn't appear to be a particularly pleasant conversation.

"What do you think that's about?" Rand asked.

Ginger looked pained. "I don't know."

His protective instincts kicked into high gear. "Want me to intervene?"

"No. Maria has three teenage sons, a husband who is not always known for his work ethic and a crew of roughnecks working for her. She can handle Conrad the same way she does all the rest."

They watched as Maria shook her head firmly and walked past Conrad, who still seemed to be pleading his case, even after Maria got in behind the wheel.

"Well, whatever he wanted, he didn't get it," Ginger observed when Conrad got in his vehicle and drove away, too.

Rand let out a low sound of agreement. "At least he's not still bothering you."

Briefly, guilt flashed across Ginger's face, but she recovered quickly as they continued down the street. Then she paused, presumably to look at the menu posted in the window. "Actually, Conrad is still texting and calling and emailing me, every day, telling me it's not too late. I can still come back to Profitt Oil."

Rand had assumed that had all stopped, and was dismayed to find it was still ongoing. Although he did understand why Profitt would be loathe to let Ginger slip out of his life. Rand felt the same way.

He leaned a shoulder against the glass. "What do you say to him?" he asked, curious.

Ginger made a noncommittal sound. "Nothing. I already answered him once, in person. There's no reason to do so again. Eventually he'll get the message."

Rand hoped that was so.

Ginger rocked forward on the heels of her boots and studied him thoughtfully. "You're not jealous, are you?"

He lifted his brow. "Should I be?"

Chapter Eleven

What did it mean if Rand was jealous? Ginger wondered, trying not to read too much into his droll retort. Especially if he wasn't the kind of guy to ever get jealous?

"No, of course there is no reason for you to be even the tiniest bit jealous." Although she knew she was playing with fire, feminine devilry made her pursue the issue. She narrowed her gaze. "Why on earth would you be, anyway?" It wasn't as if her ex had anything on the incredible man in front of her. Rand was not only ruggedly sexy in that all-man-to-her-woman way. He was funny and charming to boot.

Still not looking all that concerned, he shrugged. "Because I don't want my wife being pursued by another man."

Admiring his confidence, she reiterated, "Well, you don't have to worry about that. The only man I want is you." Realizing belatedly how that sounded, she wrinkled her nose. She hadn't meant to be so possessive, either. "You know what I mean," she added hastily.

He met her gaze, the corners of his mouth barely turning up, and waited for her to continue.

Reluctantly she did. "I mean, we're married. And hence, exclusive."

"Anything else?" He studied her, his expression inscrutable.

Actually there was. But Ginger didn't want to get into that now, didn't want to open herself up to hurt. "Yes. I'm starving." She let her glance fall discretely to her tummy, then stood on tiptoe to whisper into his ear, "And I'm pretty sure you-know-who is, too."

As always, the mention of the baby they were having united them in a common cause.

"So what are we waiting for?" He brushed a kiss to her cheek, then, hand to her waist, ushered her inside the pizza restaurant. They settled in a cozy booth in the back, and placed their order.

As Ginger had expected, their dinner was delicious. And Rand was a charming dinner companion. They finished off the pizza and salad, then lingered over a huge slice of cheesecake, topped with fresh blueberries, strawberries and whipped cream.

Aware she'd eaten her half of the shared dessert, and maybe a little more, Ginger put a hand to her tummy and groaned. "I have a feeling I'm going to regret this."

He chuckled. "You'll be fine."

He took out his wallet and put his card on the receipt tray. The waitress took off with it before Ginger could stop her.

She frowned at Rand. "Hey, I'm supposed to pay!"

He shook his head, as intent on being in charge as ever. "Really can't let you do that…"

Why did he always have to be such a man?

"Then I'm just going to owe you."

His eyes twinkled. He seemed more than ready for whatever she sent his way.

"That sounds fine." He leaned over and kissed her slowly, lingeringly on the lips. "More than fine, actually."

Ginger hadn't meant to respond, but when he dipped

his head and kissed her again, even more evocatively this time, she found herself kissing him back, just as sweetly.

When he finally moved away, a round of applause followed.

Ginger flushed at the reaction of their audience. Rand smiled even more wickedly, and then moved to kiss her again. "Playing Mr. Newlywed to the hilt, aren't you?" she commented when they finally pulled apart.

His eyes darkened emotionally. "I'm definitely starting something."

She knew he was.

She just wasn't sure where it would lead.

Where she *wanted* it to lead.

They were quiet on the drive home. Taking advantage of the blessed silence, Ginger turned her attention to the passing scenery and mulled over ways to keep the expectations they'd started their union with intact.

And only when they had turned into the lane leading to their cottage at the Red Sage, did she finally turn to him and speak what was on her mind.

"Do you think we should add sex to our marriage contract?"

RAND HAD TO hand it to Ginger. Just when he thought he was beginning to understand her, she went and laid something like that on him. "I don't know." He cut the motor on his truck.

The spring evening was pleasantly warm and serene. The sun was setting, against a backdrop of granite mountains in a blue-gray sky. Closer to the cottages, well-tended beds of red sage and a collection of other wildflowers and natives grasses bloomed.

"Do you really think we need to do that?"

Ginger inhaled a deep breath. She seemed apprehensive again. "Well…maybe." She shrugged and released the catch on her seat belt, then sat back against the seat. "It's clear we still desire each other."

He wondered if she had any idea how cute she looked in men's clothing. Or how much he wanted to unbutton her shirt right now.

"And always will."

The stubborn tilt was back to her pretty chin. "We don't know that."

Body hardening, he watched her exit the cab, her movements as graceful and feminine as the rest of her.

She reached around to open the rear passenger door. She stuck her head in, and continued her argument determinedly. "My body is going to change, and that may change the way you feel about having sex with me."

"You're probably right." Ignoring her quick look of surprise, he circled around his truck to help carry her shopping bags inside. He set them down and watched as she closed the door behind him. "Probably, as time goes along, I'm going to want to make love to you even more."

Her rosy lips took on an even more mutinous twist. "I'm serious!"

He walked around, shutting the blinds one by one, while she paused to take off her boots, then turned on the lamps, lighting the cottage with a soft, romantic glow.

If she needed reassurance, he was here to give it. "So am I." He caught her against him and stroked her hair with the palm of his hand. "You're only…what? Three months along? And already your breasts are full and luscious and spilling out of the cups of your bra."

She moaned. "Rand."

He moved around behind her until there was no space between them, nothing but pleasure. "Your tummy has this intriguing little slope." He ran his hand sensually over the baby bump.

She shuddered in response and her eyes drifted closed.

He pressed a smile into the softness of her hair. "And your thighs. I don't think they've ever been this silky." His hand slid between them. "Or the most delectable part of you, so..." He unzipped her jeans and slid his hand inside. "Wet."

She throbbed at the tender stroking of his palm. "That's because pregnancy fills me full of hormones."

"That's part of it," he murmured, turning her to face him.

"What's the rest?"

Rand tugged her jeans and panties off, and lifted her onto the counter. Body aching with the need to claim her, he stepped between her spread thighs. Their glances met. He imagined what it would be like to be with her, like this, not just until their baby was born, but forever.

"It's basic chemistry." He undid the buttons of her shirt and lavished the curve of her cheek, the lobe of her ear, her throat, with his lips and the tip of his tongue. She quivered; her full, voluptuous breasts taut against the sheer fabric of her bra. "Whenever we're around each other for any time at all, I want you, and you want me."

She caught her breath. "But..."

He threaded his hands through her hair. "No buts, Ginger. It's true." And proceeded to kiss her, again and again, until she was as hungry for him as he was for her. His head got a little lighter, his body got harder. And still their mouths meshed as he consumed what little resistance remained.

Ginger kept trying to keep her feelings out of it. This was just sex, fueled by a million different things. Except the one thing that counted. The one thing that could have made them last forever. *Love*. He hadn't mentioned it. She didn't dare. Because she knew if she let herself fall for Rand in that way, there would be no turning back. She'd want him in a way he had never been prepared to give, and that would ruin everything.

So she forced herself to concentrate only on the warmth of his touch and the urgency of his body. Desperate to feel the heat of him surrounding her and filling her body, she ordered brusquely, "Undress. I mean it, Rand. Now."

Instead he tugged off her shirt, her bra.

And brought her right back against him.

The nakedness of her inner thighs brushed against the sturdy fabric of his denim. His lips lightly moved against hers, and he kissed her until she felt her soul stripped bare. Tongue plunging into her mouth, hands moving upward to claim her breasts.

Again and again they exchanged wet, hot, hungry kisses and she welcomed him in, welcomed him with everything she had.

Catching his head between her hands as he worshiped her breasts, her thighs.

Bringing her to the edge of the counter and holding her there...plunging her into passion, then sweet rapture, as a violent shudder racked her entire body.

She tangled her hands in the silky hair at his nape, bringing him upward, forcing his mouth back to hers. And then, finally, his boots and jeans did go. And so did his briefs and his shirt. He stood there, in all his naked glory, wanting her as much as she wanted him. She appreciated all the gorgeous male muscle and whorls of dark silky hair lingering over his navel, his thighs and the most masculine part of him, before returning her gaze back to his.

He smiled.

"Ready whenever you are."

He laughed. And crushed her to him. She ached with the need to be filled, and yearned with the desire to be loved. "Now, please," she whispered.

His eyes softened. "With pleasure."

She braced her hands on his shoulders. He lifted her toward him, and up slightly, against him. Their joining was everything she wanted, everything she dreamed. She gave herself over to him, to this, the marriage she'd never imagined possible. And for one long moment, as their bodies exalted and their hearts sang, she let herself imagine that maybe…just maybe…their relationship might last.

RAND WENT TO sleep with Ginger wrapped snugly in his arms and woke at two in the morning, alone. Concerned she might be feeling ill again, he went in search of his wife. She was curled up on the love seat, a blanket across her lap, oblivious to everything but the laptop computer in front of her. He stood framed in the doorway, for a moment just taking in his new wife.

The softness of her breasts, pushed against her pale blue pajama top. Her long copper hair, tousled from sleep… her fair cheeks still bearing the glow of their recent lovemaking. She was intent on whatever she was studying onscreen, her dreamy concentration only adding to the gentle contentment that seemed to radiate from her these days. Pregnancy agreed with her. So did marriage, though he doubted he could get her to admit that. Yet.

She turned, spying him in the doorway.

He smiled, and glad for any excuse to be near her, sauntered closer. "Can't sleep?"

"Checking my email."

He went to the fridge and poured them each a glass of milk. He closed the fridge with his foot. "I thought the

Boernes weren't supposed to notify the semifinal winners until tomorrow morning."

"They're not."

"Then..." He settled beside her. "You're looking at cribs?"

Their fingers brushed as she accepted the glass he gave her. "And baby clothes. And furniture. I was trying to get an idea of what it was going to cost to outfit a nursery."

She moved the cursor to the bar along the top of the screen that showed him the other webpages she had been perusing.

"You're getting excited."

She admitted as much with a nod. "Aren't you?"

"I am. But I also know you need your sleep."

She gave him the look she always gave when anyone tried to tell her what to do, think, feel... "Uh-huh."

He grinned at her decided lack of enthusiasm. Figuring he knew just how to get her where she should be, however, he waited until they'd both finished their milk. Wordlessly he set the glasses and laptop aside, stood and swept her into his arms.

"We're not making love again," she warned.

He carried her to the bed. "I know."

But they did make love. And this time they slept, wrapped in each other's arms, until eight the next morning.

Ginger was the first to stir. She lifted her head, looked at the clock and groaned. "I forgot to set my alarm."

Aware how hard she'd been working, he kissed her brow, then eased from the bed. "Sleep in."

"I can't." But then Ginger sighed and snuggled deeper into her pillow. "Maybe just five more minutes..."

She was fast asleep by the time he was dressed.

Whistling, Rand headed for the buffet, figuring he would surprise her with breakfast in bed. He was halfway to the main house when he saw Cordelia's white Cadillac parked in front of the guest ranch office, his mother moving hurriedly inside. He had no idea what was going on, and honestly, didn't think he *wanted* to know. But when he passed the open windows, Cordelia's sweet, plaintive voice floated out to him. "I think we should do it, Josie. I think it would help."

His mother argued back. "More likely, Cordelia, it will make things worse."

And "worse," Rand knew, was something that they did not need.

Not when his marriage to Ginger was finally become as real as it needed to be. He took a detour into the building, bypassed the reception area and walked into the party-planning suite.

Cordelia was dressed in an elegant business suit.

His mother wore jeans.

Both were poring over a lot of pale pink and light blue party stuff. Wondering what the hell was up, he asked, "What's going on?"

"Nothing," both women said in unison, stepping in front of the stacks on Cordelia's desk.

The way the two moms were blushing guiltily and wouldn't quite look him in the eye said a lot. None of it good, Rand thought. He pointed to a cardboard cut-out of a stork carrying a bundle that said, Good News Is Coming Soon! He grimaced. "Tell me this doesn't have anything to do with me and Ginger."

Another telltale silence. Rand took a hard, assessing look at his mother, then another at Cordelia. He shoved a hand through his hair and exhaled wearily. He couldn't say how or why, but... "You know. Don't you?"

For a second no one said anything, no one moved. The two women seemed to know they were being presumptuous. Finally, Cordelia threw up her hands and looked at him as if he were the idiot in the room. "Of course we know. Your mother and I both knew the moment we saw you and Ginger together on your wedding day. The way she was glowing and you were strutting around like a proud papa to be!"

His mom added informatively, "An even bigger clue to us was the fact you were getting married at all, never mind so quickly, when you had both told everyone after your divorces that you were never walking down the aisle again."

Rand scowled. "If it was so obvious, why didn't you say anything to us then?" he demanded.

His mother sighed. "Because we didn't want to deter you from doing the right thing for your baby."

"And because I knew the moment I saw you with my daughter that you were the man she's been waiting her entire life to meet and fall in love with," Cordelia said.

Except he and Ginger weren't "in love" with each other, Rand thought. Not yet. Maybe not ever. And, as long as they stayed as happy as they had been the night before, he was beginning to be okay with that, too.

He shook his head, as if that would clear it, then went back to what the two women had been quarreling about when he entered. "So why were you arguing?"

Cordelia stiffened. "I want us to throw you and Ginger a surprise baby shower in the party barn."

"Not gonna happen," Rand decreed. "In fact, no more surprises of any kind."

Josie folded her arms. "I told you he wouldn't like it, Cordelia."

"Ginger won't, either," Rand added.

"Why not?" Ginger's mom argued. "You can't tell me my daughter's not happy about having your baby!"

Of course Ginger was happy; they both were—that went

without saying. It was a new life. A part of him. A part of her. What was there not to be happy about?

"She doesn't want anyone to know because she's worried they will hold it against her when it comes to business," Rand explained.

"And she's right to think that way." Josie backed up his claim. "Wildcatting is still largely a man's domain. There are a lot of people who don't want women on job sites period, never mind pregnant women."

"You faced the same discrimination?" Cordelia asked her, looking thoughtful.

Josie nodded. "Naturally, I worked around it, just as Ginger's doing." She reached over and squeezed Cordelia's arm. "I know you mean well. We all do. But you and I have to step back and give these two lovebirds the time and space they need."

"And that means," Rand concurred, "Ginger's 'news' is hers to tell whenever and however she sees fit."

Cordelia studied him with a mother's keen eye. "You really adore my daughter, don't you?"

Rand nodded. More than anyone would ever know. "So you'll do what I ask?" He looked at both mothers. "And pretend you don't know?"

Josie and Cordelia nodded in unison.

That settled, Rand headed over to the main house. He filled a to-go platter for them to share, then circled back to the cottage.

As he expected, Ginger was awake. She had a broad smile on her face.

Rand set their breakfast on the dining table. "What's going on?"

She pointed to her computer screen. "Maria and I made the semifinals—that's what! We drew Slot 9 on the Q and A sessions tomorrow!"

"That's wonderful." He crossed the room and wrapped his arms around her.

Ginger hugged him back. "Of course it's not just me." She babbled on, reaching for the can of ginger ale she'd been sipping. "Profitt Oil and your mother's company were chosen, too. But this is great. I'm officially in the running."

"Good thing I brought you some breakfast, then." He winked.

She put a tentative hand to her tummy. "Thanks, but…" She took another small sip of soda. "I think it's just going to be saltine crackers and soda for now." She rose, already in high gear. "I've got to call Maria. Get a shower. Prep for the Q and A!"

The rest of the morning went swiftly.

By noon, Rand had received a phone call, too.

Not sure how *his* news would go over, he went to find Ginger, who was sitting on the back porch, running through her data. She took one look at him and sat back in her chair. "What's wrong?"

Reluctantly he filled her in. "Dot and Clancy have asked me to sit in on the Q and A sessions."

Her brow furrowed. "I thought only three independent geologists were going to do that."

"Initially, that was the plan. Now they want an environmental engineer there to handle any issues that may arise. And since I've already vetted all the proposed drilling plans…"

She considered that with her usual cool professionalism. "Makes sense."

"Are you okay with this?" She'd worked so hard. He didn't want to do anything that could possibly throw her off her game. And having him in the room could distract her.

Ginger pushed a hand through her hair. "Would it matter if I wasn't? You've already refused to recuse yourself once."

He'd since had time to regret that. "For this round, the identities of the participants won't be hidden, unlike the way they were in the initial proposal review."

She studied him, as if wondering why he was even asking her this. "Is this new attitude of yours because we put sex back on the table? And you don't want us to take it off again?"

It was deeper than that.

Not sure she should hear that now, though, when her attention should be solely on the oil lease she was trying to acquire, he merely shrugged. "Let's just say I'm very invested in keeping peace in our family." *As well as continuing to make love to you every chance we get.* "So if this is going to make you uncomfortable in any way…"

Abruptly she looked vaguely insulted, almost irked. "No. I want you there," she responded quickly, then paused, struggling to explain. "I feel better when you are around. Safer. And I know that's odd. Not to mention totally out of character for me. Let's chalk it up to a pregnancy thing, okay?"

Damn but she was cute when she was hormonal.

Chuckling, Rand took her in his arms. "I like being with you, too."

GINGER SPENT THE rest of the day alternately feeling very confident and very anxious. To the point she was considering her options when Rand ambled in at dinnertime, carrying takeout from the local barbecue.

His gaze drifted over her. "Still can't get hold of Maria?"

Ginger brought plates, silverware and napkins to the table. "I've emailed, texted and called her repeatedly all day."

Rand filled two glasses with water and ice. "Is it possible she's on a job?"

"No." Ginger sat opposite him. "The one she and her crew were working ended late last week."

His gaze swept her thoroughly. "Maybe Maria hasn't checked her messages."

"Maybe."

He reached across the table and took her hand. "I'm sure she'll check them tonight."

Ginger hadn't felt the need to lean on a man in a long time. She felt it now. "You're right. I'm being paranoid." Deliberately, she shook off her low mood. "Maria's probably just been prepping, same as me."

He opened the paper bags and set the containers of mesquite-smoked chicken, potato salad, green beans, slaw and peach cobbler on the table.

"Looks good."

He grinned, already loading their plates. "Got to have you strong and fit for tomorrow."

Smiling, Ginger took two bites and put her fork down.

Concern lit his gaze. As always, he knew the second it hit. "Morning sickness?"

Deliberately she took a deep breath and willed the nausea away. "Or evening."

Rand took his cell phone out of his shirt pocket. "Want me to call your OB-GYN?"

The sight of him reacting like a parody of an expectant dad made her heart sing. "No. I see her next week. I'll talk to her then, if it doesn't improve." Beginning to feel a tiny bit better, Ginger leaned toward him. "You should go with me. Meet her. I mean," she added hastily, suddenly wondering if she was asking too much, "if you can."

His smile deepened. "Of course I can."

They resumed dining. Rand ate with the hearty appetite one expected of a man his size. Ginger tried her best, but still couldn't really eat anything. Finally she pushed back her chair, knowing if she didn't get away from the sight and smell of the deliciously prepared food soon…

Rand joined her as they carried their dishes to the sink. He laid a comforting hand at her back. "Can I do something for you? Make you some chamomile tea or something?"

"No. But don't worry…I'll be okay." Ginger swallowed hard. With the tips of her fingers, she blotted the perspiration dampening her hairline. "I haven't actually thrown up since that one time. I've always been able to work through it."

Determined this would not be the exception to the rule—bad enough he'd seen her hugging the toilet bowl once—she walked out onto the back porch. A nice breeze was sifting through the screens, and the mountain air was cool and bracing. She truly appreciated the beautiful scenery as the peaceful evening descended. Gradually, her pulse rate slowed. Her stomach settled.

Able to see she was finally feeling better, Rand laced an arm around her shoulders. "I'm really proud of you, you know."

The funny thing was, she was proud of him, too. Ginger turned toward him. The fronts of their bodies touched as she tilted her face up to his. She loved it when he held her like this. So tenderly and protectively. "About the job?"

He sifted a hand lovingly through her hair. "The way you handle everything that comes your way."

She splayed trembling hands across the solid warmth of his chest. "I don't know about that," she confessed. "I'm feeling pretty nervous right now."

He wrapped his arms around her, gathered her closer yet. "You're going to do fine."

He said it with such conviction she could almost believe

him. She leaned her head on his shoulder and let him hold her. "Just keep saying that."

Keep making all my dreams come true.

Chapter Twelve

Ginger stared at Maria the following morning, feeling as if the rug had just been pulled out from beneath her. "What do you mean you can't work with me on the Boerne lease?"

"I'm sorry. I really am." Maria wrung her hands. "But I have to do what's best for my family and my crew. The job I've been offered is a one-year gig. Guaranteed. Even if we were to win, which…" Doubt crept into her voice. "You know how stiff this competition is…"

Ginger thought about what she and Rand had seen in Summit the evening before. "Did Conrad have anything to do with this?" she asked furiously.

Maria shook her head. "He made me an offer. I turned him down flat, same as you. This gig came from the Southwestern Oil Company late last night."

A reputable midsize firm, not involved in the bidding in Summit County.

"Part of the deal was I start today."

Ginger held up her hand. "I understand." And the hell of it was, she did. Having a family changed everything.

"I'm sorry, Ginger. Really I am." Maria pivoted and hurried down the sidewalk to her truck.

Ginger stood there, watching numbly as her ex-drilling partner drove away.

Rand came up behind her. "What are you going to do?"

Good question. "At the moment? Try not to lose my breakfast." Ginger whirled and went back inside the cottage.

Only a step behind her, Rand stood just inside the front door. Ginger stared at him. Although she wasn't scheduled to appear until much later in the day, he had to be there within the hour. "Don't you have to be going?" she snapped.

"If you need me…"

She lifted a hand. "I'll be fine. Really." Hand to his shoulder, Ginger pushed her husband out the door.

He hesitated on the other side of the threshold. "Call me if you need me."

Ginger nodded. But they both knew she wouldn't. Like it or not, this was something she had to figure out for herself.

Hours later, she was still struggling with the recent turn of events.

She drove into town, fighting morning sickness every step of the way. Aware it was Conrad's turn to defend his company's proposal, she avoided the lawyer's office where the meetings were being held, and stopped by the pharmacy instead. Sweat gathered at her hairline as she perused the aisles.

As always happened when she wanted to appear incognito, a clerk appeared at her side. "Are you feeling all right? You look a little green."

No surprise—she felt awful. Ginger took another deep, enervating breath. "I was looking for some spearmint lozenges or lemon drops."

"They're with the candy." She led Ginger two aisles over and gave her a sympathetic smile. "If you need anything else, let me know."

Ginger nodded. She picked up one package of each, another bottle of chilled ginger ale and a sports drink containing electrolytes.

She paid for her purchases and went back out to her truck, drove to the park down the street from the attorney's office and sat, with the windows open, letting the spring breeze blow over her. Eyes closed, she breathed in through her nose, out through her mouth. Until finally the symptoms subsided.

Eventually, Ginger opened her eyes. Another disaster averted. Now all she had to do was get through the Q and A.

RAND KNEW THE moment Ginger walked into the conference room to face the Boernes, their attorney and the four-member panel that she was in a bad way.

He doubted anyone else knew what was wrong, thanks to the cheerful smile she had plastered on her face.

Unfortunately, given what he had already heard that day, he knew her dismay was only going to get worse.

Dot Boerne began. "First of all, Ginger, we want you to know that Clancy and I loved your proposal. You came up with a drilling plan that was not only the most cost-effective of all the proposals we received, but did not disturb the parts of our land we hold most dear."

Ginger smiled. "I'm glad you liked it."

"Unfortunately we understand that you've had some bad news. That your drilling partner, Maria Gonzales, has dropped out of the competition and taken her crew to another job."

For a moment Ginger looked taken aback. Recovering, she squared her shoulders and pushed on with her usual confidence. "That's true, but I know I can find replacement workers who are just as talented."

Clancy Boerne grinned and nodded approvingly. "In fact, you've already done so, haven't you?"

Ginger blinked. Clearly, Rand thought, she didn't know what Boerne was talking about.

The older gentleman continued. "Profitt Oil has offered to step in. And given that you've worked for them in the past—"

"Where did you hear this?" Ginger interrupted pleasantly.

"Conrad mentioned it when his team was in here earlier today."

Rand watched as Ginger nodded, her expression grave. "I'm sorry you were given that information. It's incorrect. Yes, I was asked to go back to work for the company, but I have refused, and will continue to do so."

Rand relaxed in relief.

"Then…?" Dot persisted.

"I still want to do the job, but it's going to mean finding another crew…"

The Boernes nodded their understanding, but they weren't happy. More questions followed. Though it was clear by the time the Q and A session ended that Ginger had lost whatever edge she had walked in with.

Rand followed her outside during the brief break that followed.

Hands on her hips, she glared at him. "You knew?"

He nodded. "There was no way I could warn you."

Briefly, hurt and dismay flickered in her eyes. She looked ready to break into a string of roughneck-ready words. "Of course you couldn't."

Rand kept his physical distance. "Your ex-husband is a horse's behind, but I still have a job to do here, and I have to be fair."

Ginger nodded, then pivoted sharply and headed for her truck. Rand followed, hard on her heels, his urge to protect her stronger than ever. "Where are you going?"

She jerked open the driver's door, threw her briefcase in and climbed behind the wheel. "Exactly where you'd think. To find my no good ex-husband and give him a piece of my mind!" She drove off.

Torn between his duty to hear the last Q and A of the day—which happened to involve his mother's company— or see to his wife, Rand went back inside. The choice was easy. "Sorry about this, but my wife needs me," he said frankly and without apology. "You all are going to have to carry on without me."

It DIDN'T TAKE long for Ginger to spot Conrad's Porsche. It was in front of the steakhouse on Main Street. She parked her truck and went inside. Conrad was seated at the bar, bourbon in hand. He had a smug, happy look on his face.

Although she was still fighting waves of ever-increasing nausea, she was determined to have this out with him here and now.

She tapped him on the shoulder and he slowly turned around. "Hey, darlin'…" His voice was slurred. It was as if he, too, knew he had lost his bid for the Boerne oil lease.

"Were you responsible for Maria getting a job with another oil company?"

Conrad squinted thoughtfully, as a garlicky smell Ginger might have appreciated under any other circumstances floated in from the dining room.

Her ex took another sip of bourbon as she swallowed and tried not to breathe in. "I might have mentioned to a colleague or two that she was awfully good—had to be if she were going to partner up with you—and relatively inexpensive, too. Compared to some of the other outfits around."

Conrad's needling smile deepened, as did the resentment in his gaze. "I also might have mentioned there was a very narrow window, in which to steal her away from all this

Boerne ranch business. Why?" He chuckled mirthlessly, his wounded ego showing. "Did your friend back out on you? Let you down, the way you let me down? Or…wait. Have you come here to beg my forgiveness in front of all these people, so I'll bail you out of the mess you're in?"

Ginger's fists knotted at her sides. It was all she could do not to punch him in the face. "You conniving, mean-spirited snake…"

Conrad set his glass down and rose slowly. "It was a mistake to tell the Boernes that you would never under any circumstances work with me or anyone at Profitt Oil again."

His bourbon-scented breath was even more unpleasant than the garlicky smell. Ginger reeled backward. "How c-could you…?" she sputtered.

Conrad raised his cell phone. "Because their attorney telephoned me to verify, as soon as you left the room," he said, leaning in, his low voice turning even uglier.

With effort, Ginger held her ground. "So what?"

"So now it's my turn to ruin your business prospects," Conrad threatened.

Without warning, Rand came up behind Ginger and stepped protectively in beside her.

His timing stank.

Unaware that the last thing she wanted—or needed—at that particular moment was to have her husband come in to fight her battles for her, Rand put a gentle hand on Ginger's waist. Furiously, she shook off his touch. The people in the bar, which were mostly oil men, began to chuckle.

"I've got this," Ginger hissed as yet another wave of smells—this time some sort of pan-seared fish—wafted in from the dining room.

Muscle working convulsively in his jaw, Rand stayed exactly where he was, but did not attempt to touch her again.

Determined to further the show they were now putting

on for everyone in the steakhouse bar, Conrad tilted his head in a mocking manner. "Well, isn't that sweet. Looks like the little woman—or should I say wife?—has emasculated you, too."

More chuckles. A gasp. And a swift, shouted prediction of trouble to come.

"But then, that's what you do, isn't it, darlin'?" Conrad turned back to Ginger. "You marry a man with great oil company connections and you use him to try to get into the executive ranks. Only in this case, the oil company you have your eye on eventually running is helmed by a woman. So you probably think your master plan will be even easier to execute."

No one who knew Josie Corbett-Wyatt McCabe would ever think the female wildcatter was able to be pushed around.

Ginger shook her head vehemently. "I never wanted to take over Profitt Oil," she informed everyone in the room.

"Really? 'Cause it seems like you did a pretty good job of showing me up within the company, when you were my wife. And then when my father and I finally understood your game, you divorced me and lassoed him." Conrad pointed to Rand.

Aware her husband was holding on to his own temper by the slightest of threads, Ginger retorted, "That's not why I married Rand."

"Yeah?" Conrad downed the rest of his drink, then followed it with a short, resentful laugh. He leered at her. "Then why did you marry him in such a great big hurry if it wasn't to somehow influence what happened from here on out? Are you going to tell me you love him? 'Cause I don't buy it. There's something else going on here."

There was. But Ginger couldn't reveal it, not with the Boerne decision still hanging in the balance. Sickness overwhelmed her as another wave of assorted food smells assaulted her. Aware she was about to embarrass them all, she told Conrad grimly, "You're a jerk, you know that?"

And then, unable to fight it a second longer, she leaned over and threw up all over his fancy rattlesnake boots.

THE PROBLEM WITH throwing up, after two entire days of trying not to throw up, was that Ginger couldn't seem to stop. Even after her stomach was emptied, the dry heaves continued.

That was how she ended up in the emergency room cubicle at Summit hospital, with Rand at her side, slowly but surely easing her humiliation and making sure she got everything she needed.

Two bags of IV fluids and some anti-nausea medicine later, she was finally able to catch her breath and turn her attention to the loving man beside her.

She wasn't the only one who looked as though they had just been through hell. Rand's usual calm was shattered, his expression turbulent, his jaw tight.

Ginger met his eyes. "Sorry I let it get that far."

"Probably no sorrier than Conrad's boots."

His joke broke the tension, and she laughed. "Somehow I have the feeling my ex is not going to be bothering us again."

Rand's eyes glittered with humor. "Probably not."

Their gazes meshed. Ginger squeezed Rand's hand.

"I know what I said earlier, but the truth is, I'm glad you were there. It helped, knowing you had my back."

"Even if you didn't want me to actually step in and defend you?"

Ginger nodded.

Tenderness radiated from him. "I'm glad I was there, too." He tightened his fingers on her.

Another heartfelt moment passed.

A nurse, who had been standing there quietly waiting, shook her head and muttered, "Lovebirds." With a wink of approval, she exited and promptly returned with the E.R. doctor, Thad Garner.

The nurse wheeled the ultrasound closer to Ginger's gurney as Dr. Garner asked, "You two heard the baby's heartbeat yet?"

Rand and Ginger shook their heads.

"Well, you're in for a treat." The doctor smiled as the nurse spread gel across Ginger's tummy, switched on the machine, then handed him the wand. On the television screen, they saw what looked like liquid moving waves. Then, as he continued moving the wand over Ginger's belly, the shape of a tiny baby appeared. It was one thing to know you were pregnant via test results—it was another to actually see your little one nestled snugly in your womb. Ginger gasped in amazement. Head, body, fingers, toes… All were there.

Tears of happiness flooded Ginger's eyes. Wonder filled her heart. And then the sound. *Th-thump. Th-thump. Th-thump.* Their baby's steady, strong heartbeat echoed through the room.

"It's too early to tell if it is a boy or a girl yet…" Dr. Garner said cheerfully. He grinned at the emotional parents-to-be. "But all looks good." He printed out a photo for them, then handed it over. Rand and Ginger perused it together joyously.

Dr. Garner continued, more seriously, "But we need to do something about the nausea, so that you don't get this sick again, because hyperemesis is definitely not good for the baby. I talked to your OB-GYN over in Marfa. We agreed you need to take it easy for a few days. And we're sending you home with some anti-nausea medication, to take as needed. It will make you sleepy, so don't drive or operate heavy machinery while you're on it, okay?"

They nodded and thanked the doctor. He slipped out. The nurse removed the IV from Ginger's arm, and Ginger was free to dress. She looked at Rand gratefully. "You've been really great today, you know that?" Tears misted her vision.

"Hey." Gazing down at her tenderly, he traced a thumb beneath her eye and kissed her cheek. "That's what husbands are for."

They didn't talk much on the drive back to the cottage. The medication had indeed made Ginger sleepy, and she dozed most of the way. She was so wobbly upon arrival that Rand picked her up and carried her through the door to their cottage, and all the way to their bed.

Some of their neighbors saw and chuckled.

Ginger moaned and rested her head against his broad chest. "They probably think it's some honeymoon thing."

Rand grinned. "Yet another benefit to being married." He set her down gently, then went to help her ease off her boots. "Pajamas now? Or later?"

"Actually…"

He waited.

Ginger pushed herself up on her elbows. "You're not going to believe it, but…I'm actually hungry."

Rand sat beside her. He aimed to please. "What do you want?"

Ginger grunted in frustration and rested her head on her bent knees. "What do I want? Or what can I have?" They were two different things.

He kissed the top of her head. "The first."

Ginger tested her steadiness, and found, now that she'd been sitting up a minute, she felt a lot better. "Well…" She squinted, thinking. "I'd kill for my mother's homemade chicken noodle soup."

Rand rose. "I could ask her to make some."

Ginger caught his wrist before he could spring into action. "No. I can't push my mom away for being too intrusive one moment and then summon her at the first sign of trouble. It's not fair."

Rand scrubbed a hand across his jaw. "I don't think she would see it that way. I think she'd be grateful to help."

Ginger went to the bureau and pulled out a pair of loose-fitting cotton pajamas. "That's the problem. Once my mom starts, she doesn't know how to stop helping."

"And that's the only reason you don't want your mom here, because she's been too pushy in the past?"

Leave it to her husband to see even her most closely guarded anxiety. Reluctantly, Ginger admitted to herself that the being-too-close-for-comfort thing with her mom sometimes went both ways. Deciding on impulse that she wanted a shower, too, Ginger got out a clean towel and washcloth, and stashed them in the bathroom.

"If I were to see my mom right now, I think the fact I'm pregnant would come spilling out. And I don't want to tell our families that way. I want it to be a totally happy occasion, with everyone we love gathered together."

Their glances met in the bathroom mirror. "Kind of like the engagement-party-slash-wedding announcement we missed?"

"Yeah." She paused, studying him, too. "Do you get that?" She knew it was sort of corny.

"I do." He lingered nearby while she brushed her teeth. "We may not have started out our marriage in the most orthodox way, but we can publicly start out the pregnancy in a way that mirrors the joy we feel."

Ginger blotted her mouth. "And it's only a few more

days. Once the Boernes make a decision—" and she knew what her immediate work future held "—then you and I can start thinking about how and when we're going to tell people our 'news.'"

RAND WAS JUST hanging up the phone when Ginger came out of the bathroom fifteen minutes later. She was clad in her favorite pair of loose-fitting pink-and-white-striped pajamas that buttoned up the front. She had a white towel wrapped around her head, and her feet were bare. She still looked tired, but her color was better and she seemed to be moving more energetically.

"Who was on the phone?" Ginger asked, settling in a corner of the love seat.

"Our moms."

She paused in the act of unwinding the towel from her hair. "They heard?" Her cheeks turned a little pinker.

Noting how good she smelled—like the citrusy soap and shampoo she used—Rand sat beside her.

"Everyone in town heard."

She groaned and covered her face with her hands. "What did you say?"

"The same thing I plan to tell everyone—that your illness was a combination of exhaustion, stress and dietary indiscretion."

Ginger worked a comb through her hair. "That sounds ladylike."

"Doesn't it?" He winked and they exchanged grins. "Anyway," Rand pushed on seriously, "they both know you're fine." *And that the baby is fine, too.* He cleared his throat. "And the doctor said you needed rest. So back to what we were discussing before you showered—what you're going to eat tonight. I say we do what your mother suggested and refer to the list of acceptable foods the E.R. doctor gave us on discharge and figure it out on our own."

Ginger did a double take. "Whoa. Wait. Cordelia actually said that?"

Rand nodded. He'd been surprised, too. "With a great deal of difficulty, but yes, she did allude to the fact that I'm your husband and I need to start helping you with things like this, and vice versa, if we are ever to be the kind of team—"

Rand stopped in midsentence, swore mentally, aware he had almost said, *The kind of team our baby is going to need us to be.*

Ginger finished combing the tangles from her hair. "What?" She prodded him to finish. "What did my mom say?"

Knowing now was not the time to add to his wife's stress, by letting her know he had already confirmed their happy news to their moms without her knowledge, he said instead, "The kind of team that all good marriages are. Or something like that. It was a little…"

"Preachy?"

He winced diplomatically. "That's not the word I would use."

Ginger laughed and rolled her eyes. "Well, my mom is right, on this, and probably many other things, as well, loathe as I am to admit it. You and I do need to figure this out on our own." She rose once more.

Aware she was supposed to be resting, he blocked her way to the kitchen. "But what you want is chicken noodle soup?" Gentle hand to her arm, he guided her right back to their bed.

Ginger shrugged, sighed and obediently climbed beneath the covers. "It's what I always have when I've been sick."

Good to know. "Then chicken noodle soup it will be." He brought in a sleeve of crackers and some ginger ale in the meantime. "I thought about making toast…"

"You're right." She smiled at him. "Better to be safe than sorry."

His heart going out to her, Rand kissed her forehead and then headed back to the kitchen to see about rustling up some of the soup she craved.

WHILE RAND SEARCHED the cupboards for a can of soup, Ginger ate a couple of crackers, took a sip of ginger ale, then lay back against the pillows and closed her eyes. It had been a long few weeks… Before she knew it, she was fast asleep.

She awakened several hours later to the most delicious smell.

For a moment she was back home in her childhood bed, her mom in the next room, and the most wonderful sense of well-being came over her.

And then she became aware of her wedding ring, and she remembered how she had come to be in this situation. And the tears that had been held back burst free and rained down, full-force. And that was, of course, when Rand walked in, looking handsome as ever. "Hey." He took her in his arms and held her until the storm passed. "You haven't even tasted my soup yet…."

She cupped his face. His skin was warm and his evening stubble rasped against her palms. "You made me soup?"

"I asked your mom for the recipe and she was kind enough to email it to me."

"That's it? My mom just sent it to you? She didn't offer to make it for us or insist on running over?"

Rand gave a slow shake of his head. He turned his face

into her palm, and brushed his lips across the center. "No, she just told me how to make it, and I have."

He left again and Ginger fell silent. Had she finally gotten through to Cordelia, after all these years of enduring her smothering ways? Or was there some other reason her mom was suddenly more hands-off than usual?

Her husband returned, tray in hand. "Although," he cautioned cheerfully, "no guaranteeing the results. I'm a griller, not a soup maker."

Ginger sat up against the pillows. "I'm sure it will be great."

"Well, I cheated. I didn't make the noodles from scratch. I used store-bought." He pulled up a chair, flipped it around and sank onto it.

Once he'd fit the tray across her lap, Ginger dug her spoon into the rich golden broth, redolent with carrots, celery, chunks of white chicken and plump egg noodles. She blew lightly, then lifted the spoon to her lips. "Where did you get them?"

Rand's eyes roved over her lovingly. He appeared to like what he was seeing despite the fact her hair was sleep-rumpled and still damp. "My mom. She was still in town, having dinner with her team. So she stopped at the grocery on the way home and dropped the stuff off."

Ginger took a bite, then another. The soup was just what she needed. She smiled. "That was nice of her."

"It was."

Another pause. "Was she mad at you for skipping out of her Q and A?"

Mad at me? "No." Rand sobered. "Everyone understood. When a man's wife needs him, the man goes. End of discussion."

Her throat tightened a little. "You don't think that she thinks I was trying to undercut her in any way? Professionally or otherwise? By not having you there to back her and her team up, if need be—"

"Or disagree with them," Rand interjected. "No. My mom didn't mind. Although, as it turned out, there weren't any environmental issues for most of the semifinalists, since pretty much everything had already been covered in my initial analysis and environmental impact reports. Basically, any competitor with problems on that score didn't make the cut."

Relieved, Ginger ate more soup. "So when will the Boernes decide?" she asked eventually.

"They are going to take two or three days to confer, then they will let everyone know one way or another with a phone call from their attorney. Which, as it turns out, is a good thing for you—" he flashed her a heart-stopping grin "—since you and our baby are supposed to spend the next few days resting." He hesitated, still scrutinizing her. "So? How is the soup?"

"Really good," she decreed.

Blue eyes narrowed. "But not as good as your mother's?"

Of course he would put her on the spot. Knowing it was some kind of test—that he wanted to see if she would lie—she eventually sighed and said, "It's not better or worse, it's just different." She spooned up the last of his soup, savoring every bite. "Homemade egg noodles taste different than store-bought."

"Next time," he promised, rising to take the tray from her.

As soon as he'd set it safely aside, Ginger grabbed him by the front of his shirt. Grinning, she hauled him against her. "*This time* is great." She raked her fingers through his dark rumpled hair, not sure what she would have done this past month without him. Not wanting to find out, either.

"Just in case I haven't made myself clear." She matched

his wickedly sensual look with one of her own. "You've been a wonderful husband, a wonderful father-to-be, a wonderful everything...."

His mouth quirked and she brought him nearer still, intending only to share a quick, easy kiss. Her plan went awry the moment their mouths meshed.

He cupped his hand at the back of her head and kissed her again, slowly and masterfully. Helpless against the tidal wave of feelings, she gave herself up to his embrace.

His arms came around her as he joined her on the bed, threw back the covers, and stretched out beside her. He dropped his head and kissed her again until she moaned, until the point of breathlessness. Her body was humming with need. "Rand," she whispered, wanting the safety and heaven only he could provide.

Briefly he lifted his head. "Is that a yes?"

She laughed and trailed her tongue across the powerful curve of his shoulder. "Heck, yeah."

He grinned. Taking in a sharp breath, he threaded his hands through her hair and tipped her head up to kiss her.

The make-out session continued, as hot and heavy as ever. Impatient, they rolled onto their sides, facing each other. Still kissing, caressing. Her hands slid to his fly, unsnapping, unzipping. His fingertips slid beneath her pajama top, tracing the round shape of her breasts, the shadowy valley between, before finally finding and caressing the tight tips. An arrow of desire shot through her. Lower still, she was so wet. And still, they kissed and touched, stripped each other naked, and then they kissed again, until they gasped in tandem pleasure. Not satisfied with her shaky moan, he slid down her body. Nestled between her thighs.

She writhed against him in exquisite torture. She caught his head. "Now, Rand..." She wanted him inside her.

Rand knew their culmination would be better if he took

his time. He also knew there was much, much more he wanted to give. So he simply smiled and went on a little tour. The flat of her belly, the indention of her navel, the insides of her thighs. Then lower still, kissing and caressing her until she was clutching at him, making soft little whimpers for more. He demanded everything of her, until she willingly gave it, and the distance that sometimes cropped up between them, completely faded.

And still he kissed and fondled, and let her ardent response seduce him, heart and soul. He blazed a trail over her sensitive spots, giving her exactly what she wanted and needed, until she arched and cried out.

"Now, you," she insisted.

And as it turned out, he couldn't deny her that, either. Heart racing, he lifted her on top of him, eager for mutual gratification. Slowly, gently, he guided her onto him. She raised herself up a little, wrapped her hand around him, and took him deep. Their eyes met as they moved in perfect synchrony. And then they kissed again, his thumb sliding over the spot where they joined. She came again, which he liked, because it meant she felt so much…he felt so much…and he immediately followed her. Satisfaction roared through them and, still trembling, she pressed her face to his throat.

Aware of everything that had changed between them—and all that, to his frustration, still hadn't—he continued to hold her close. She clung to him, murmuring her pleasure, and eventually sliding right back into sleep. A deeper contentment—coupled with a soul-deep worry—followed. And as he held her, Rand couldn't help but think of the look on his wife's face back in the steakhouse bar.

For a moment when publicly pressed about why she had married him, she'd had that deer-caught-in-the-headlights look.

Rand hoped she didn't feel as trapped as it had momentarily seemed. Because the truth was, their marriage was the best thing that had ever happened to him. He hoped by the time their baby was born, she would feel the same way.

Chapter Thirteen

The following evening Rand walked in the door and did a double take. His gaze swept the nicely set table and cottage living area. Both were neat as a pin. He followed his nose and headed straight for the stove. "What's all this?" He peeked at the chicken roasting in the oven.

Proud of her handiwork, Ginger flashed him a sassy look and brought out a salad from the fridge. "What do you think it is?" She shook the bottle of homemade vinaigrette and poured it over the mixture of fresh raspberries, almonds and spinach leaves, then carried it to the table.

Pleasure lit his face. "You're cooking dinner for me?"

Ginger winked and went back to fill the serving platter. "I know. Amazing, isn't it?"

He washed up and helped her carry everything to the table. He paused to hold out her chair for her. "You were supposed to be resting."

Ginger wrinkled her nose. "For me, this *is* resting."

Smiling affectionately, he sat opposite her. "That's probably true."

"And we do have to eat," she noted as they filled their plates with tender slices of chicken and roasted root vegetables. "So what better than food I've prepared for us?"

"Did I bring the right woman home from the hospital?"

Ginger grinned. "Funny."

"Really. All kidding aside, what's going on?" Sobering, he paused to search her face. "Did you find out you won the bid?"

Tension stiffened her spine. "No. There's no news on that front."

"Then…?" He met her gaze and the air seemed to crackle around them.

Ginger had promised herself that even though their situation was changing due to the baby, they would not have to alter anything about themselves. When the truth was, they had already begun to change, for the better. Aware they were on the brink of some sort of mutual epiphany, she shrugged. "I thought about everything you've done for me since we got married. All the food you've brought in, the laundry you pretty much finished by yourself, not to mention going clothes shopping with me and bolstering my spirits."

"And the sex," he interjected, his eyes gleaming mischievously. He lifted her wrist to his lips and tenderly kissed the inside. "Don't forget the great sex."

Tingling with need, Ginger returned his flirtatious glance. "There's no way I'm forgetting the great sex. Not. A. Single. Minute. Of. It." She punctuated each word with evocative meaning.

He grinned and leaned across the table to kiss her on the mouth. "Exactly what I want to hear."

When they eventually pulled apart and went back to enjoying their meal, Ginger continued. "I'm serious, though. I think you've been a much better husband to me than I've been a wife to you." She felt guilty about it.

"That's not true. You're carrying my baby."

"Our baby," Ginger corrected thickly.

And it was a part of her and a part of him and a precious symbol of all their life would one day be…

"You're right." Rand's glance drifted over her barely discernible baby bump. "It's *our* baby." Contentment flowed between them as their eyes met.

Their serious mood intensifying, Rand bared his soul. "You've also made me realize there's a lot more to life than work and causes."

Ginger relaxed, realizing she wasn't the only one who was being transformed. "Such as?"

"Home. Family." He started to say what Ginger thought might have been "love" then changed it to simply, "All this."

Ginger rose to clear the table and retrieve the dessert she had made. Over her shoulder she said, "I do like our life together."

He caught up with her at the kitchen sink and took her in his arms. "Me, too." His mouth hovered over hers, and they kissed.

When they came up for air, she said, "Chocolate cake..."

"Sounds good." He undid the first several buttons on her shirt. "But it can definitely wait."

She closed her eyes and sighed as his lips made an evocative tour of her throat, collarbone and the sensitive spot behind her ear. Hands clutching his shoulders, she caught him with a kiss on the jaw. "We've so begun to think alike."

He lifted his head and captured her gaze. "Which, in this instance, is a very good thing."

Rand swept her up into his arms and carried her into the bedroom. Ever so gently, he let her down beside the bed. Toed off his boots. Removed his socks. Reaching up behind him, he tugged his shirt over his head in one very smooth, easy motion. Her mouth went dry at the sight of him in just a pair of low-slung jeans.

Her eyes roamed his satin-smooth skin and strong muscle. "Keep going."

His lips quirked. The jeans went. So did the boxer briefs. Oh, my.

His breath rasped. "Now you."

Eyes holding his, she undressed slowly. One by one, everything came off. Shirt. Bra. Socks. Jeans. Panties. His heated gaze made a slow, thorough tour of her.

"We're good?"

He grinned. "So good."

The next thing she knew, he had pulled her against him. She loved the feel of him even as she loved the ragged groan she wrenched from his chest. Her hands were everywhere. So were his. Their kisses were long, languid, passionate and sweet.

Breathing erratically, they landed on top of the covers. He palmed her breasts. She clutched his biceps and arched up into him. And still they kissed and kissed. Already cradled by her open thighs, he slid into her. She cried out, shuddering in pleasure. And then there was nothing but the two of them, this moment, their future beckoning as powerfully as their present. His strokes were strong and slow, making her groan, making her want. She quivered and trembled against him, letting him know how very much she needed the oblivion and wonder he offered.

"Now, Rand, please…"

He gripped her hips. "You first…" His raspy declaration was all it took. Her body exploded in sensation, and as she came, she took him along with her, their locked gazes as steadfast as their hearts.

An hour and one more lovemaking session later, they were cozily ensconced on the screened-in porch. Clad in pajamas, eating slices of chocolate cake and scoops of homemade vanilla ice cream. He bussed the top of her head. "You are an amazing chef."

"Thank you." She grinned and kissed him back.

He savored the very last bite. "This is, without a doubt, the best dessert I have ever eaten."

Seizing the opportunity, Ginger playfully feigned affront. "That's the one thing I didn't actually make."

Rand went still. Bemused by the way he constantly felt he had to protect her tender feelings, Ginger chuckled. "Actually, I made that, too."

Let off the hook, he gave her a chiding look, then kissed the bridge of her nose. "And she jokes, too."

Finished with their desserts, they set their plates aside and cuddled together on the porch swing. Aware she needed to unburden herself to someone, and she wanted that someone to be her husband, Ginger eventually admitted what had been nagging at her all day. "I think I'm going to lose the bid."

Rand lifted a dissenting brow. "First of all, you haven't lost it yet," he reminded her. "But, *if* you do, it'll be because of—"

Ginger jumped in to list all the mitigating factors. "Maria's defection, not to mention the fact that I don't have the skill set to build an entire wildcatting company from scratch." Exhaling, she turned her troubled gaze to his. "Because if I did, let's face it, I never would have allowed my ex to sabotage me the way he did."

Rand pushed the swing into a lazy comforting rhythm, as matter-of-fact as ever. "For the record, I didn't see that coming, either."

But that wasn't all that was bothering her. She studied Rand, wanting his reaction to this, too. "The point is, if Dot and Clancy don't choose me to do the drilling on their land, I'm going to have to make a decision whether to pursue another job with someone else. Or—" and this, she knew, was even trickier "—hold off looking for something else until after the baby comes."

Rand shifted her onto his lap. "You know I'll support you in whatever you do. Especially if you find you really like being a mom and—" he squinted, waiting for her reaction "—want to take time off to have another baby, too."

His words were a shock, all right. Ginger put her arms around his shoulders. "Whoa. *What?*"

"Well…" Mischief lit his midnight-blue eyes. "Sometimes it's good to get all the baby-making out of the way at once, if you're planning on resuming a career, and/or you want to give a child a sibling close in age, so they'll have a playmate growing up."

His logic was both convoluted and oddly reasonable. Trying not to get too caught up in the fantasy of what it would be like to have a real long-lasting family with Rand, instead of the temporary situation they had both agreed upon at the outset of their marriage, Ginger bit her lip. "That was the one thing I always lamented, not having a brother or a sister."

He rubbed his thumb across the curve of her lower lip. "I always wanted a sister, but after five boys, mom and dad said they were done."

She grinned wryly. "I imagine their hands were pretty full." With five sons, all as handsome and smart and full of life as Rand.

He shook his head, remembering what appeared to have been a fun-filled childhood. "You have no idea." He cleared his throat and regarded her with choirboy innocence. "Anyway, if you decide you want to do this again, I want to go on record here as saying I'm all in."

Ginger shifted, feeling the resurgence of his desire—and hers. "All in?" she teased.

His laugh was low and seductive. "Most definitely all in."

Aware what would happen if they continued to be that close, Ginger slid off his lap and carried their dishes to the kitchen. "Don't you think that would be a problem?" she said over her shoulder. "I mean, if we were to do that, we wouldn't be married by then. According to our agreement, we'd be divorced."

He stepped in to help with the dishes. "We could always get married again. Or stay married and put it in our infamous contract."

Ginger nudged him with her shoulder. "Hey, that contract is going to save us a lot of grief over the years."

His hands encircled her hips, and he turned her to face him. "If we ever finish it."

Ginger shivered in the night air coming through the open windows. "We'll finish it," she promised.

He combed his fingers through her hair. "You really think so?"

"I know so," she returned softly. Because she really wanted this temporary marriage of theirs to work. And even though she knew they were getting ahead of themselves, turning the practical arrangement into an increasingly romantic one, she still wanted them to succeed. Not just as parents, but on every level.

GINGER DIDN'T KNOW whether it was the loneliness of the cottage after Rand had gone off to work, or the thought of waiting another day before finding out which company had won the lucrative bid…or just the fact she was pregnant. All she knew was that she missed her mom and needed to see her. And there was, Ginger knew, only one cure for that.

So just before lunch, she went over to the Red Sage business office. Her mom was in the party planning suite, looking as pretty and personable as ever. She paused in the doorway, aware her mother still had every reason to be irked with her. "Got a minute?"

"Always." Cordelia put aside the stack of invitations she had been working on. She perused Ginger with her usual mixture of affection and worry, then finally said, "You look good."

Ginger felt good.

Accepting her mom's wordless invitation, she sauntered in to take a seat on the other side of her mother's desk. Ginger smiled, suddenly wishing she could break down and tell her mom everything that had been going on. She wanted to tell her how hormonal and nauseated and overjoyed and overwhelmed she had felt the past three months. But she couldn't. Not when she and Rand had decided they would tell their families about the baby, all at once.

Aware her mother was still perusing her closely, Ginger shrugged. "I guess I've got that honeymoon glow."

"That must be it," Cordelia mused in return.

"Well, that and some extra sleep the past day or so," Ginger couldn't resist adding.

Another sharp-eyed maternal glance. "Over your stomach upset?" she asked gently.

Ginger nodded, comforted to know her mother still cared. "Which brings me to my next point. I wanted to thank you for giving Rand your famous chicken noodle soup recipe."

Cordelia's eyes lit up. "How did it turn out?"

"Good." She smiled back, then felt obliged to admit, "Well, not as good as yours, but it was still very comforting."

Cordelia interjected, "It's the thought that counts."

"Yes, it is." Ginger sighed, knowing that Rand wasn't

the only one who deserved better from her. Still looking her mom in the eye, she pushed on, "I want to apologize. I haven't been very cordial to you, as of late."

Cordelia lifted a delicate hand. "You had reason to be annoyed with me," she said. "I shouldn't have just quit my job and taken one here without speaking with you first."

Ginger rose and moved closer. She leaned against the desk, needing to be near. "That's the thing, Mom. I was wrong about that, too. You don't need to ask me for permission to do what you want to do, any more than I need to ask you. We're both grown women. We can make our own decisions."

Cordelia stood and embraced Ginger in a warm, heartfelt hug. "I just want you to be happy."

Relieved to no longer be quarreling, Ginger hugged her mom back. "I am, Mom." For the first time, in a really long time. "I really am."

Cordelia squeezed her hand. "I know, honey. I see that in you and Rand. And that makes me feel like I can go on with my own life in a way I really haven't been since your dad died."

Ginger blinked. "Are you trying to tell me you're dating again?"

"I'm trying to tell you I'm going to start." She smiled serenely. "Seeing you with Rand has reminded me what it's like to be in love with someone, really in love, and what it means to make that leap of faith, and share your life with that person."

Was that how they looked to others? Ginger wondered, astonished.

Cordelia told her, "I want to be married again and have a fuller, more satisfying life. And seeing you with your new husband is what's convinced me to do so."

"SHE THINKS WE'RE in love," Ginger told Rand over dinner that same night.

He studied her, as if not getting the guilt they should both feel.

"We both know that love never entered into our decision to marry," Ginger pointed out.

Another inscrutable look. Another long, thoughtful pause. "That's true." He frowned. "But—"

Ginger's cell phone rang. It was the notification she had been waiting on. She swallowed and picked it up, her hand trembling with apprehension. "Ginger Rollins." She listened, her spirits sinking like a stone. "Yes. I understand." She ignored Rand's concerned look, then managed to say, "Thank you. I appreciate that." She closed her phone, not the least bit consoled to discover her bid had come in fourth overall. "I didn't land the job. Your mother's company did."

"I'm sorry."

"Me, too," Ginger admitted. Had she not been married and expecting a baby, she probably would have been devastated. "But if it wasn't me," she said, determined to be a good sport despite the setback, "I'm glad it was her."

A knock sounded on the door. Josie McCabe was on the other side of the screen. Squaring her shoulders, Ginger smiled at her mother-in-law and motioned her in. "Congratulations."

Rand glared at his mom in exasperation.

"Couldn't you have given Ginger a little time to lick her wounds?" he demanded.

Josie came forward briskly, businesslike as ever. "No, I couldn't. I need to ask Ginger what I've been wanting to ask her for weeks. I want you to come to work for my company. And I want you to work with me on the Boerne project. And, Rand, I want you to come to work for me, too."

Rand gave his mother a wary look. There was an undercurrent between them that Ginger could not decipher, but clearly something was going on between them.

"Why?" Rand asked tersely.

Josie gave Rand an enigmatic look back. One that confirmed there was something else going on, some other reason besides Ginger's and Rand's business acumen.

Josie lifted a hand, index finger up. "Because Wyatt Drilling has always been a family company, handed down to me from my dad." Her finger count went to two. "You are the only one of my children who is remotely interested in the oil business on any level." She raised a third finger. "I think having an environmentalist on board to advise us on each and every project is a good idea. And four—" she made the appropriate gesture "—I think the three of us working together to run this company will be a very good thing."

Josie's smile encompassed both Ginger and Rand. "I don't expect an answer right away. I know you have to think about it, but when you are ready to sit down and hammer out the details, let me know, and we'll do it."

"I don't appreciate the timing, Mom," Rand told her rather brusquely.

Josie gave Rand another telltale look that seemed to speak volumes. "Just think about it," she said as she headed out the door.

When they were alone again, Ginger asked, "Did you have any idea that was coming?"

Rand helped her clear the table. "None."

Aware she hadn't had this nagging sense of being deliberately excluded in a familial tiff since she'd been married to Conrad, Ginger put a pot of decaf coffee on to brew. "Well, it doesn't make sense to me," she ruminated, still wondering what Rand—and Josie—weren't telling her.

"Why would your mom be in such a rush to have us both working with her?"

Rand shrugged and averted his gaze. "You're a tough, talented competitor. She probably doesn't want anyone else to hire you."

There was still something missing. Ginger continued pacing. "I mean, it would make sense why she'd want to bring me into the family company as soon as possible if she knew about the baby. But there's no way she could know about that. Unless…" Ginger studied the peculiar expression on Rand's face. "Did you tell her?"

A long, reluctant pause followed. "I didn't have to," he conceded finally. "She and your mother had already figured it out."

The news was like a bucket of ice water poured over her head. *"When?"*

He barely looked at her. "From the moment they saw us on our wedding day. They saw how you were glowing. Noticed how fast and determinedly we were getting hitched—despite the fact we had both vowed after our divorces that we would never say 'I Do' to anyone again." He spread his hands wide, as if it were no big deal. "And they figured it out."

"And told you."

He gave her a longer, narrow look. "No. I walked in on them arguing about whether or not to throw us a surprise baby shower a week or so ago."

Lovely. "And didn't see fit to tell me? *Any* of you?"

"Your mother wanted to confront you." His eyes remained steady on hers. "I forbade it."

"Why?"

Frustration turned the corners of his lips. With the tone of a man who was never expected to explain himself, he returned, "Because you were already fighting morning sickness and under so much stress at work. I didn't want you to end up in the hospital."

Ginger huffed. "Which I did anyway."

"Unfortunately."

Ginger stared at him, wondering how everything could turn so awful, so fast. Hands knotted at her sides, she moved closer. "So all this time, the three of you were—what?—humoring me."

He glared down at her, said mildly, "Protecting you. And yes, we were."

Tears misted her eyes. "At your insistence," she clarified.

His jaw set. "It's my job, as your husband."

She spun away from him, overcome with a horrible sense of déjà vu. "It's your job to tell me the truth!" she cried.

"And I am."

"Now!"

Another silence fell, even more fraught with tension than the last. There was suddenly so much wrong with their situation, Ginger didn't know where to start. Her gaze jerked back up to his eyes.

She supposed the best place to start was where the trouble began. "I can't accept your mother's job offer."

Acting as if this were all hormones again, instead of a fundamental breakdown in their relationship, he stared at her in weary resignation. "Why not?"

Ginger went back to what had upset her at the end of her conversation with her own mother that day. The willful deception that had paved the way for the entire past month. "Because," she sighed, irritated she had to explain this to him, too, "your mother just asked because she thinks our marriage is a real one."

His expression grew stonier.

"I mean, she does, doesn't she?" Ginger persisted. "You didn't tell our mothers *that part* without me, did you?"

"No, of course not."

"So they think we've made a real, lifetime commitment to each other?"

"I assume so, yes."

"Then we have to set the record straight," she reiterated, going back to what she'd been trying to tell him over dinner. "And explain to them that our marriage is nothing but a temporary arrangement for business reasons."

He folded his arms across his chest. "What if I want it to be more than that?"

Tension knotted her gut. In an effort to gain control, she returned to her usual businesslike attitude. "You know our agreement," she told him.

And she knew her promise to *herself,* to never again be in a relationship where she was humored and betrayed, the way she'd been in her first marriage.

Rand stood his ground. "I know our *initial* agreement."

Meaning what? The fact they'd become closer gave him license to do whatever he pleased as far as she was concerned? "Our marriage is not a forever kind of thing," she reminded him stubbornly, refusing to delude herself into believing otherwise.

His face took on a brooding expression. "You're saying you still want a divorce as soon as we have the baby?"

Did she? In a perfect world, no. But he had more than proved this wasn't utopia. Not even close. She had to be practical. If she stayed, he would break her heart. And maybe their baby's heart, too. Swallowing the lump in her throat, Ginger ran a weary hand through her hair. "I'm saying I'm tired of the pretense. I don't want to walk around every day feeling like a liar. Because that's not who I am. And it's not who you are, either, Rand." That much she knew.

He exhaled roughly, looking as ticked off as she felt. "You're right about that."

Their anguished glances meshed and held. "Then you understand we have to tell our parents the truth about why we really got married, that we were never as wildly and passionately in love as we pretended."

He lifted a brow, challenging, "Or ever will be for that matter?"

Ginger didn't know what to say to that.

In the end it didn't matter.

Rand simply looked at her, a world of hurt and disappointment in his eyes. "Point made," he said quietly.

And then he walked out.

Chapter Fourteen

"And that's it?" Michelle asked from across the law firm conference table two days later, her expression inscrutable. "Rand just grabbed his laptop and left?"

Ginger nodded and settled even deeper into her chair, aware she hadn't felt this miserable in her entire life. "I haven't seen or heard from him since. Hence, I wanted to let you know we would be coming to you for a marriage dissolution instead of a marriage contract."

Suddenly she paused. "You don't look surprised." Ginger had half expected the happily married attorney to give her a lecture on sticking with it and seeing the problems through. Instead, Michelle was calmly making notes on the yellow legal pad in front of her.

"So what was it like before the big blow-up the two of you had?" Michelle asked.

"Great, actually," Ginger admitted, a little mystified about that, too. How was it that things had gone from so wonderful, to so bad, that quickly?

Calmly, Michelle continued to take notes. "You were working on the terms of your marriage contract?"

Ginger nodded. "Trying to anticipate—and solve—any problems that could possibly come up in the future. Not that there were many in the present. We just naturally seemed to click as roommates. And lovers."

Wow, had they ever clicked as lovers, she amended silently.

"But then what happened in the bedroom had never been the issue between us," she continued, aware she needed a sounding board, and the quietly analytical attorney in front of her was as good as any. "That was good from start to finish."

Michelle looked up. "And Rand seemed happy then, too?"

"Very. I mean, I'd never seen him so relaxed and…content, I guess. Before we hooked up, he was always using his passion to fight for one environmental issue or another. Then, when we realized the baby was on the way, everything sort of changed." She sighed. "Our focus shifted more to each other and making things work than on either of our business goals. And once that happened…everything just seemed to fall into place."

"Even when you had small differences of opinion on the actual terms of the marriage contract, the two of you were trying to hammer out?"

"That's correct." Ginger exhaled. "As furious as I was with him over not telling me that our mothers knew we were expecting a baby, I never thought he'd decide to end things just like that." Ginger studied the levelheaded family law lawyer. "But you're not at all surprised, are you?"

Michelle put her pen down. "You want me to be frank?"

"I do."

"You and Rand were and are the exception to the rule."

"In what way?"

"Most people enter into marriage thinking it's going to be some fantastic fairytale. They don't understand— or want to understand—what you and Rand intuited from the get-go. That marriage *is* a business, albeit a very personal one."

Ginger blinked, still listening intently.

"In either situation, you first decide to throw in together. Then you draw up the contract. When, how, where you're going to proceed. The day you get married compares to the day you go to the secretary of state to actually register your new business."

Ginger reflected on the official legal start to their new venture. "That was an incredibly happy moment."

Michelle smiled. "It is for everyone because it's the beginning of the honeymoon period."

That had been wonderful, too.

"But then the real work begins." Michelle sobered. "By-laws for the business—or in your case, the actual terms of the postnup and marriage contract—are drawn up. And let me tell you, no one ever agrees about those. It's always a difficult process. There are always subtle but significant differences of opinion. In business, quarrels concern how much to spend on advertising or how much staff to hire..."

She cleared her throat. "However, in marriage, it's usually an emotional issue, such as whether or not you should quit pretending to be in love and tell your families the real reason you got married when you did. Or whether Rand should have told you the moms had guessed you were pregnant, instead of moving to protect you the way he thought was right in that moment."

It was clear Ginger and Rand had serious disagreements about those issues. But also true that their quarrel didn't seem as significant today as it had when it had occurred.

Ginger studied the happily married woman opposite her. "You're saying I should cut Rand some slack?"

Because Rand's gallantry is one of the things I love best about him? One of the things I've come to count on the most?

The savvy attorney smiled knowledgeably. "I'm saying that whether in business or marriage, everyone always plans for when things go wrong." She paused to let her words sink in. "No one ever plans for what happens when everything goes *right*."

"SO IT'S TRUE?" Josie said to Rand when he tracked her down at the Boerne ranch two days after her visit to the cottage. He could see that surveying and staking was already under way. "You're ending another marriage?"

Rand scowled at his mother. "I was hoping you'd give me some tender loving care."

"Nope. Fresh out of that."

"Seriously?" he quipped.

Josie looked him squarely in the eye. "I'm not going to sugarcoat it for you, son. You're being an idiot."

Rand followed his mother over to her pickup. "She's not ever going to love me, Mom."

Josie grabbed a couple of bottles of electrolyte drinks from the cooler, and handed one to him. "Do you love her?"

What difference did it make? Rand wondered as he worked the cap off and took a long, thirsty swallow.

His mom quenched her thirst, too, then continued looking at him the way she had when he'd brought home a note from school saying he had misbehaved in some fashion. She had always wanted an explanation from him first, before passing judgment. She wanted one now, too.

Rand exhaled in frustration. "We were supposed to see our family law attorney today to hammer out the final details of our postnup and marriage contract. The appointment was made weeks ago."

"Okay. And...?"

"Ginger sent me a text saying she was planning to attend without me, and that when she was there she was going to let Michelle know where things stood."

"Which is where?"

"I don't know. Over?"

Josie arched a brow. "Shouldn't you be asking her that instead of me?"

"As you know, she's pregnant."

"So?" his mom asked.

"I don't want to argue with her. Or upset her."

Josie rolled her eyes. "And she couldn't possibly be upset now, with the two of you not speaking to each other."

Rand returned the sarcasm with equal vigor. "Is there a point to this cockeyed lecture?"

An indignant sniff. "I want to know why you aren't at that meeting, too."

"Because I do not want to go over there and be put in a position where I have to defend myself for doing what was right in the first place."

"I see. So, bottom line, you're afraid Ginger might disagree with you in front of the attorney, and hurt your feelings?"

Why did his mother persist in misunderstanding the entire situation, as well as his motives? "Because I'm—"

"Afraid?"

"—pretty damn sure that Ginger is going to want to continue our marriage only as a means to an end. And while I might have thought it was an acceptable idea in the first place, I don't anymore. Hence, I'm not going to pretend everything is right as rain, and drag out a union that is bound to end in another colossal failure." Sighing roughly, he raked a hand through his hair. "I'm not like you and Dad and my brothers. I'm not good at figuring out who to spend the rest of my life with, Mom."

His outburst was met with thoughtful silence. Finally his mom tilted her head and probed gently. "I'm interested. How did you come to that particular conclusion?"

Rand grimaced. "Easy. I married one woman who wanted me to give her everything money could buy."

"And when you didn't, that marriage ended, rightly so. Although had you asked me, I would have told you from the get-go she was a fortune-hunter."

Rand turned a glance skyward and pleaded for patience. When he finally had it, he looked back at his mother. "Then I married a second woman—"

"Who doesn't want your money or even any sort of family nepotism when it comes to her career, either."

Rand paused to decipher that. "Ginger turned you down?"

Josie nodded. "In an email. She said as much as she would love to work with and learn from me, she couldn't in good conscience accept a job offered her only because of family connections that were going to end anyway."

His spirits plummeted yet again. "Did you disagree with her? Try to get her to change her mind?"

"No."

He squinted. "Why not, if you believe in her?"

His mother let out a reluctant breath. "Because Ginger is right. If you two don't work this out, she would never be happy working with me."

So much for the pep talk he'd wanted, even if it had been as off-base as the rest of his life. He folded his arms in front of him. "Well, we're not going to work it out."

Another contemplative pause. "What makes you so sure of that?"

Same reason as always. "Because Ginger's elusive to the core."

"Independent to a fault." Josie helped heap on the criticism.

"She's never going to let me give her anything," Rand railed. "Not commitment or security or—" He stopped.

His mother smiled and, guessing exactly where he'd been going with that rant, delivered her final blow.

"Love?"

GINGER WAS BACK at the cottage, trying to figure out what her next step was going to be, when a knock sounded at the door.

Rand stood on the other side of the screen door.

He looked resolute. Handsome. Serious.

Her heart turned over in her chest at the sight of him standing there, clad in one of the button-down Oxford-cloth shirts she had once enjoyed wearing so much.

"Hey," she said softly before she could stop herself or think of a better opening to what she wanted and needed to say.

He smiled at her and, lips set stubbornly, opened the door and strode inside the honeymoon cottage where they'd begun their married life. Languorously, he crossed to her side. "How did your appointment with Michelle go?"

It was a simple question. Packed with emotion, beneath the masculine reserve.

She let her glance caress the long muscular legs, encased in soft faded denim, his equally worn boots. Remembering how much she loved every part of his strong, tall body, she returned her gaze upward, over the hard musculature of his chest and neck, to his face.

She took a bolstering breath. "I wanted to talk to you about that." Wanted to do a lot of things, in fact.

Another flicker of indiscernible emotion appeared in his midnight-blue eyes. He came closer, wrapped an arm around her waist, then put a silencing finger to her lips and said gruffly, "First, I need to say a few things."

Ginger splayed her hands across his chest. "Okay."

He looked at her with sincerity and regret. "I haven't

been honest with you. So in a way, you're right. I have disrespected you this whole time by not leveling with you."

It helped to have him admit that, even as the knowledge filled her with fear. Ignoring the sudden wobbliness of her knees, Ginger urged, "Go on."

"I know what I said about it being only a temporary, heat-of-the-moment kind of thing the first time we landed in bed together."

She had pretended the same.

"But the truth is," Rand confided hoarsely, gazing into her eyes, "I never wanted a no-strings, easygoing affair with you. I was just humoring you, and telling you what I thought you wanted to hear."

Her heart clenched. "As a means to an end."

"Maybe." He paused, reflecting. A mixture of mischief and irony turned up the corners of his lips. "Because I did want to see you again and I figured downplaying what had happened between us was the only way that was going to happen."

His deadpan humor was infectious. "You're probably right about that," Ginger returned dryly. She'd been shaken to the core by the intensity of the passion they'd felt. Still was.

Rand tenderly cupped her face in his large hands. "But mostly it was because I let my pride and my fear of failing at another relationship get in the way."

Ginger tipped her head up to his. "I've been apprehensive about putting myself out there again, too. Which is," she explained, "the only reason I ever considered a continuous string of one-night stands with you. Because I was afraid to look any more forward than the moment we were in."

"But the truth is—" he admitted, his voice a sexy rumble "—from the very first time I set eyes on you, I knew in my gut that I was never going to be satisfied with that. I'm a one-and-only-one-woman kind of a man. And the one woman I want in my life is you, Ginger Rollins-McCabe."

Tears slipped down her cheeks as she thought about how much time they had lost, how abandoned she'd felt the past couple of days. "Then why didn't you tell me?"

He searched her face with quiet intensity. "Because I knew how much you prized your independence."

"Maybe not so much anymore."

He shushed her again. "I'm not finished." His voice caught. "You've got to let me get this out."

Her throat aching with pent-up emotion, she nodded.

"I don't want to end our marriage," he said, flattening a hand on her spine and bringing her closer. "And it's not because we're likely to be taken more seriously in business if we stay hitched, or because it's what our families want, or even more importantly, because a two-parent home will be good for our baby…or any other children we may also choose to have—"

She grinned at the realization he was thinking ahead, again.

"It's because there is no other woman in the entire world for me. It's because," he continued in a gruffly tender tone that lit her soul on fire, "you bring a joy and a contentment and an excitement to my life in a way that no one ever has before. I love you, Ginger Rollins, with all my heart." He bent his head and kissed her sweetly. "And I have from the first moment we hooked up."

The last few pieces of her broken heart mended at the realization they'd been on the same track all this time, they'd just been too stubborn and too wary to admit it.

Ginger kissed him back. "That's good to hear." She was crying in earnest now, so happy she felt she would burst. She wreathed her arms about his neck and went up on tiptoe, getting closer yet. She slid her fingers through his hair, wanting, needing, so much. But needing to give back, too. Her breath caught in a little hiccup. "Because I've learned a lot the past couple days, too."

Rand listened intently, seeming to know that she had a lot to get off her chest, too. Bolstered, she told him with quiet honesty, "I thought if we ran our marriage with the levelheaded efficiency a good business utilizes, that we could somehow protect ourselves from any future disappointments. But I know now, that's not true. Every facet of life is messy and emotional." Her lips trembled. "In the end, all the ups and downs and working things out, is what makes a relationship so strong. The struggle to get it right is what makes us grow, and I very much want to grow old with you."

She tilted her face upward and kissed him again; he returned the caress just as lovingly. Then, with a contented laugh, she pulled back long enough to admit, "Which is why, I've now realized, I could never quite bring myself to finish that darn marriage contract. Because I sensed our life together was always going to be a work in progress. That we'd always be able to find a better, fairer, more loving way to do things. And that the day we ever declared ourselves 'perfect'—"

"Was probably the day to go back to the drawing board?" he teased.

Ginger's low chuckle mingled with his. "I haven't said it, up till now, but I'm saying it today with all my heart and soul. I love you, Rand McCabe." And to prove it, she kissed him yet again, even more passionately this time.

"I love you, too." Rand hugged her fiercely, then buried his face in her hair. "So much."

They clung together, bound by so much more than marriage vows and a baby on the way. "So we're good?" Ginger murmured as the gladness in her heart grew by leaps and bounds.

"More than good," he decreed firmly. "Ecstatic."

Epilogue

Six months later...

"So what do you think?" Ginger asked, scrutinizing the newly hung sign. "Did it turn out the way you imagined?"

Rand appraised the bronze placard hanging from the curlicued metal arm just above the door: Rollins & McCabe, Environmentally Sound Oil Exploration. He turned to her and grinned. "It's exactly the way I imagined it. No," he corrected, pausing to kiss her tenderly, "it's even better than I thought it ever could be."

"I know what you mean." Ginger rubbed her swollen belly as the two of them walked inside the office that housed their consulting business. The four-room space on Main Street, in Summit, Texas, was outfitted with a reception area, an office for each of them and a conference room. "We've already accrued quite a client list."

Ginger contracted out her services and engineered petroleum drilling plans for clients. Rand did the environmental impact reports, and made sure their client's interests were protected, in terms of their land. Companies like Wyatt Drilling and other small-to-midsize oil companies brought in the teams of roughnecks and did the actual oil exploration and recovery. It was an arrangement that worked well for everyone, and gave Rand and Ginger the freedom and independence they both wanted.

They hadn't ruled out the possibility of one day joining Josie McCabe, at Wyatt Drilling, but for now this setup suited them all just fine.

"How are you feeling?" Rand asked.

Ginger stretched some of the tightness from her spine, felt the baby kick in response, feisty as ever. "I'm fine."

Rand lifted a questioning brow, reading her as expertly as ever.

Reluctantly, Ginger relented and told him the rest. "My back hurts. It's been aching all afternoon." Aware it was time for them to call it quits for the day, she reached over and turned off her computer.

"Then why didn't you say so?"

"Because I feel like all I do is complain about— Ouch!" She paused.

Panic warred with the excitement on his handsome face. "Is it time?"

Ginger wished. She was so tired of being pregnant, tired of feeling hot and bulky and continually hormonal and out of sorts. Although Rand kept insisting she had never looked lovelier…

Patiently, she circled around to join him. "Not for a few more days. You know th— Ouch!" She grabbed hold of the edge of the desk and doubled over in pain.

"You're in labor."

Was she?

The tight rubber band of pressure circling her entire midriff said, yes, this was indeed a contraction. But one contraction, as she'd found out the hard way, did not mean she was in labor.

She relaxed as the sensation passed. Feeling a little foolish, she straightened. Rand hovered protectively close, ready to spring into action the moment she said the word. Their eyes met and she shook her head. "I don't want to go to the hospital." She moaned, remembering the excitement, followed swiftly by humiliation and letdown. "The false alarm we had last week was embarrassing enough." She'd been so sure. They both had. Only…

Rand wrapped a comforting arm around her shoulders. He kissed the top of her head. "It happens a lot. And you know what the OB staff said. Better safe than sorry…"

Ginger remembered. Still… She turned to kiss Rand's chin. "We can wait a little bit. Time the contractions and then—"

Without warning, she felt something running down her leg. More pressure. More liquid. All of it puddling mysteriously at her feet.

Rand looked at her feet, then at her face, then back at the floor. He seemed as stunned and overjoyed as she felt. "Your water just broke, didn't it?"

Ginger laughed to cover the onslaught of fierce building pain. "I knew all those birthing classes we've taken and that internet research you've been doing would come in handy," she panted.

"I'll get the suitcase," he said quickly.

Wincing, Ginger grabbed his biceps and held on tight. "It's already in the pickup," she huffed.

"Then I'll get the truck."

Again, Ginger shook her head. "How about we both walk to the parking lot together?"

"You're sure?" He was already locking up with one hand, phoning the obstetrician with the other.

"Positive," Ginger said, for once happy to cede over all control to her adorable husband. She leaned against him when he wrapped his arm around her, savoring his warmth and his strength. "I want you by my side every step of the way."

And he was. Through the short drive to the hospital, the check-in, the labor and the birth. The doctor even let Rand do the honors and cut the umbilical cord.

It was only when they were situated in the mother-baby suite that the three of them were alone again. Ginger in the bed, Rand next to her, their precious little baby girl, happily fed, and cuddled against their chests. They looked down at her gorgeous halo of Rollins-red hair and McCabe-blue eyes. She had Ginger's nose and Rand's stubborn chin. And was seriously, the most beautiful baby that either Rand or Ginger had ever seen.

They snuggled contentedly as the newborn finally drifted off to sleep. "So it's official?" Ginger whispered to Rand. "We're going to name our little darlin' Jasmine Josie Cordelia McCabe?"

He grinned tenderly, pausing to kiss both momma and baby. "We are."

"Our mothers are going to like that."

"They sure are."

Ready to share their excitement, Ginger smiled. "So what do you say we conference-call both our families and introduce them, via Skype, to our first—"

"But not last—"

"—child."

Rand got the laptop and set up the camera and microphone. "Of course, we don't have to decide the exact number of kids right now. We have all the time in the world to work on—" he waggled his brows suggestively "—that."

Ginger couldn't wait to make love with him again.

"That's what I like about you," she teased. "Always

thinking ahead." *Always taking every opportunity to love me, and let me love you back.*

They kissed again. Hearts bursting with joy, they called their families to give them the happy news.

* * * * *

Look for RUNAWAY LONE STAR BRIDE,
the first title in Cathy Gillen Thacker's
brand-new miniseries, McCABE MULTIPLES.
Available July 2014,
only from Harlequin American Romance!

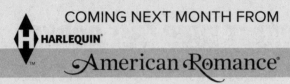

REQUEST YOUR FREE BOOKS!
2 FREE NOVELS PLUS 2 FREE GIFTS!

HARLEQUIN®

American ★ *Romance*®

LOVE, HOME & HAPPINESS

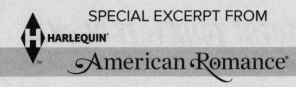
"These are your babies?"

She nodded, and he suddenly felt dizzy. The woman he loved was a mother, and somehow she'd had four children. This perfect four of a kind was hers.

It wasn't possible. He felt weak all over, weak-kneed in a way he'd never been, his heart splintering like shattered glass.

"Damn, Ash, your family… You haven't told them."

"No, I haven't."

A horrible realization sank into him, painful and searing. "Who's the father?"

She frowned. "A dumb, ornery cowboy."

"That doesn't sound like you. You wouldn't fall for a dumb, ornery cowboy."

"Yes, I would," Ash said. "I would, and I did."

He looked at the tiny bundles of sweetness in their bassinets. Two girls and two boys, he presumed, because each bassinet had colored blankets—two pink, two blue. Two of each. He felt sad, sick, really, that the woman he adored had found someone else in the nine months she'd been gone. He felt a little betrayed, sure that the two of them had shared something, although neither of them had ever tried to quantify exactly what that was. "He really is dumb, if he's not here taking care of you," Xav said, and it had to be the truth or she wouldn't be living with the woman with the wicked swing, who'd tried to crush his cranium. "Ash, I'll marry you, and take care of you and your children," he said suddenly, realizing how he could finally catch the woman of his dreams without even appearing to be the lovestruck schmuck that he was.

If anyone was father material, it was he.

Don't miss the final book in
Tina Leonard's
CALLAHAN COWBOYS *miniseries!*